The Paynesdown Road 5

The
Paynesdown Road 5

DEAN HUNT

Copyright © 2025 Dean Hunt

The moral right of the author has been asserted.

Apart from any fair dealing for the purposes of research or private study, or criticism or review, as permitted under the Copyright, Designs and Patents Act 1988, this publication may only be reproduced, stored or transmitted, in any form or by any means, with the prior permission in writing of the publishers, or in the case of reprographic reproduction in accordance with the terms of licences issued by the Copyright Licensing Agency. Enquiries concerning reproduction outside those terms should be sent to the publishers.

This is a work of fiction. Names, characters, businesses, places, events and incidents are either the products of the author's imagination or used in a fictitious manner. Any resemblance to actual persons, living or dead, or actual events is purely coincidental.

Troubador Publishing Ltd
Unit E2 Airfield Business Park,
Harrison Road, Market Harborough,
Leicestershire LE16 7UL
Tel: 0116 279 2299
Email: books@troubador.co.uk
Web: www.troubador.co.uk

ISBN 978-1-83628-397-3

British Library Cataloguing in Publication Data.
A catalogue record for this book is available from the British Library.

The manufacturer's authorised representative in the EU for product safety is Authorised Rep Compliance Ltd, 71 Lower Baggot Street, Dublin D02 P593 Ireland (www.arccompliance.com).

Printed and bound by CPI Group (UK) Ltd, Croydon, CR0 4YY
Typeset in 11pt Garamond Pro by Troubador Publishing Ltd, Leicester, UK

For Lisa

1

THATCHAM, ENGLAND, 1986

'You've never done anything, have you?' Mrs Drayton, the school secretary, said to me as I trailed behind her in the corridor.

She had appeared in my classroom with a pair of horn-rimmed glasses dangling from a chain around her neck. After speaking with my teacher, she pulled on her glasses and squinted towards my seat in the back corner, and she asked me to follow her.

'Mrs Walker didn't know who you were either,' she said, as she led me past the library. 'We thought we knew all the new 11-year-olds. Goodness knows how you've managed to avoid detection.'

'You must be very...' She frowned while she searched for the right word. 'You must be very timid.'

We continued in silence, across the courtyard to the main school building, and up two flights of stairs to her office.

'You have an important telephone call, apparently,' she said, handing me the loose telephone receiver.

The black curly cable extended across her desk. 'Hello?' I said anxiously into the mouthpiece.

'Jamie? Is that you, love?'

I recognised her kind voice immediately. 'Yes Nan, it's me.'

'Jamie, you'd better come home, love,' she said. 'It's your Grandad. Your Grandad's dead. Tell your teacher what's happened. You should come home now.'

I said, 'Alright Nan, I'm coming,' but she'd already gone.

Mrs Drayton must have heard everything. The stern expression had melted away and when I gave her the phone back, she spoke in a soft voice. 'Come back to class, Jamie. Collect your things and I'll let Mrs Richards know you're going home.'

We returned walking side by side, and when we arrived, she peeled away to the front of the classroom and whispered in Mrs Richards' ear.

Hushed conversations broke out on the far side of the room. I didn't look up, but I felt all eyes on me as I went back to my seat, pulling on my coat and fumbling my books and pens into my bag.

Mrs Richards stopped writing on the board to look over. I expected her to say something, but when she didn't, I decided not to wait, and I hurried out between the rows of desks.

Outside, the streets were quiet and wet from the rain we'd had that morning, and my thoughts turned to Grandad as I kicked my way home through the gloom and puddles.

When I turned onto Paynesdown Road, I crossed over

between the parked cars. From the opposite side of the road, I saw Mrs Higgins at number 129, spying on me suspiciously from behind the curtain of her upstairs window.

Her beige-painted cement house stood out from the others in the road with its pretty wooden flower boxes hung beneath each window.

The discarded kitchen sink and stripped-down motorbike left to rust in the garden next door sat uncomfortably next to her finely manicured lawn and sculpted flower beds, and I didn't doubt for one minute she'd complained to Nan and everyone else in the street about the junk left out in her neighbour's garden.

Nan would often say, 'If you want the whole estate to know something, all you've got to do is tell that woman.'

A postman whistled to himself as he overtook me and cut through a puddle on his bicycle. He glided up onto the pavement and his brakes squealed as he ground to a halt.

I put my head down to get past him and at the bend in the road, I saw Larry's chocolate-brown car parked outside the garages across from his house, sat among tufts of grass growing up through cracks in the concrete.

Larry lived alone at number 105. He'd been friends with Grandad for years. They'd had a regular get-together every Thursday when they'd walk down to the post office, collect their pension, and then continue on to The Swan for a drink. In the summer holidays, I'd be allowed to tag along and, for some reason, Grandad always seemed to be kinder to me when he was with Larry.

As I went past, it occurred to me that Nan might not have told Larry yet. Larry would undoubtedly be sad when he heard the news, but I also knew he would now be scared.

I walked on to our house. Freya's house on the opposite corner stood dark and deserted and her heavyset tabby cat prowled across their empty driveway where her dad usually parked his car.

Freya would have been curious and concerned why I'd been pulled out of class, but with a deep resentment burning in the pit of my stomach, I pictured her dad laughing and celebrating with his friends down the pub, when he heard that my grandad had died.

I pushed through the gate to the rear of our house, and I let myself in the back door.

Grandad's fully dressed body lay there on the kitchen floor, turned on its side and facing away from me. I didn't expect to find him there and from the moment Nan had told me to come home, I'd convinced myself his body had already been taken away.

Closing the door behind me, I held the door handle to steady myself before slipping my shoes off.

Through the archway, Nan got up from the dining room table, leaving a tall man behind. He had his back to me and was partially obscured from view, but for all that, I could tell it was Doctor Reynolds.

'Oh, Jamie,' Nan said to me as she walked over, 'I'm sorry, love.'

She was no taller than me, and every bit as skinny, and when she pulled me into her tiny frame, I breathed in her scent, lily of the valley soap.

After she'd released me, she stared down at her husband and said, 'He was supposed to be making me a cup of tea, but he keeled over and died instead.'

'Nan,' I whispered, 'I'm sorry about Grandad.'

'That's alright, love,' she said with sad eyes and a slight shake of the head. 'He was a troubled man and he's at peace now.'

She returned to the table and sat next to Dr Reynolds, who busily filled out a yellow form with an expensive-looking gold pen.

'Hello, Jamie, I'm sorry for your loss,' he said, lifting his head for an instant before returning to his paperwork. Streaks of grey around the ears of his otherwise immaculate head of mahogany-brown hair had appeared since I saw him last.

'Will you make us a pot of tea, love?' Nan asked as she lit a cigarette.

I navigated around Grandad's body to fill the kettle at the sink, and then traversed around him again to empty out the teapot.

At the end of the kitchen, our two Jack Russell dogs, Stan and Ollie, sat curled up in their basket, seemingly unaware of what had happened even though Grandad's body lay no more than a few feet away.

As the kettle rumbled to a boil, I crouched down to stroke them. Stan didn't stir, but Ollie enthusiastically raised his head and wagged his short stub of a tail.

Dr Reynolds came over and knelt down next to Grandad. He took his time and inspected the body with precise and carefully considered actions.

I busied myself and tried not to watch, and by the time he'd finished, the kettle had boiled and I'd made the pot of tea.

'No tea for me, thanks, Jamie,' the doctor said as he returned to the table and picked up another form. He added, 'Which funeral home would you like to use, Betty? I'll make the arrangements for you if I can use your phone?'

She took a long thoughtful pull on her cigarette as she pondered the question. 'Mr Rossi, please, Doctor,' she said finally. 'He's been sizing me and Bill up for years and he'd be devastated if I sent him to old man MacFarlane. The phone's through there, in the hall under the stairs.'

The doctor forced a weak smile as he got up.

'Dr Reynolds,' Nan said after him with a sense of urgency, 'we mustn't forget, you have got everything arranged for Bill, you know, he wanted to donate his body for research.'

From the door, Dr Reynolds said, 'Don't worry, Betty, it's all taken care of. Bill made his instructions very clear, and he signed all the necessary paperwork. I'll make sure the appropriate steps are taken, but you must realise they will keep Bill's body for quite some time. It could be quite a few months before it's returned for a funeral.'

After Dr Reynolds had left, I stayed with Nan at the dining room table.

Lost in her thoughts, she fell back in her chair and gazed out the window.

She smoked and we both drank tea until, unexpectedly, she said, 'He's going to miss the big fight tomorrow now. He was looking forward to that.'

From my position at the table, I had a clear view of Grandad's face. He did look peaceful, his eyes closed as if taking his Sunday-afternoon nap.

His hair had fallen out of place, and I'd never seen it that way before. Lying on his side, numerous long strands on top had come away from his head and they resembled the crest of an exotic bird.

Every day he had followed the same ritual. He'd get out of bed and come downstairs to the kitchen mirror. He would methodically slick back his full head of thick grey hair using his pale-blue plastic comb. I never understood why, but after combing it once and with everything neatly in place, he would repeat the process and comb it back again.

'Nan, did he like me?' I asked.

'Yes, of course he did, love,' she said a little too forcefully. 'He didn't mean to be the way he was, but he just wasn't very well, that's all.'

'What was wrong with him?'

'Oh, I don't know, love,' she said, unwrapping the cellophane from a new packet of cigarettes. 'I don't think anybody did. When you were young, they took him away to this place, this type of hospital place. They did all kinds of things to him. They gave him electric shocks that he absolutely hated, and put him on different courses of tablets that just turned him into a zombie. Those doctors were supposed to help him, but they did nothing but make him worse. He hated it there. They were cruel bastards, the lot of them, and every time I went to see him, he begged me to get him home.'

'What happened?'

She tilted her head to one side to keep the smoke from her eyes and lit the cigarette she'd been holding. 'I tried to get him released. I tried and tried, but they wouldn't have it. I argued with them for weeks, but each time they'd send me away and tell me it was for his own good.'

'So how did he get out?'

'He escaped,' she said, exhaling a plume of smoke. 'Climbed out of a window in the middle of the night and got out. He'd told me when he'd do it and where he'd be, so I asked Larry to drive me up there and we picked him up and took him to your Aunty Florence's.'

'Did you get in trouble?'

'No, love. They came round here a couple of times looking for him, but I said I didn't know where he was. He hid at Flo's for a couple of weeks.'

'Down in Hayling Island?'

'No, she was still in London then. Luckily, Dr Reynolds had moved to the Thatcham surgery by that time, and when he heard about it, he came to see me. I explained what was going on, and he wrote a letter saying he should be officially discharged. Your grandad came home and that was the end of it.'

The story had taken me by surprise and after absorbing it, I felt the need to say something more. I said, 'It feels strange talking about him when he can't hear us.'

She put her teacup back on its saucer and caressed my cheek with the back of her hand. 'The truth is, love, it's been that way for years.'

Ollie limped over and jumped up into Nan's lap. Nan studied Ollie's eye and removed a tissue from her cardigan sleeve to wipe away the residue weeping from it.

'I think this is getting worse, you know,' she said to herself as she screwed up the tissue. 'We need to get you back to the vets again, don't we?'

I interrupted to ask, 'Did Grandad start to get poorly when you had to leave London?'

'No,' she said, 'but it did start to get worse then. It was a gradual thing. It didn't happen overnight, but it was around that time that it started to get a lot worse, after your mum and dad had died.'

I leant over my cup, twisting it back and forth.

She said, 'There's something we must do.' Ollie jumped from her lap as she got up and she went to the drinks' cabinet behind me.

She slid back the glass pane and took out a bottle of whiskey.

'I know I shouldn't really do this,' she said, unscrewing the bottle and pouring a few drops into my tea. 'Just a little drink to see him on his way.'

'Is that the whiskey he would drink on Christmas Eve?' I asked.

'Yes, love, he did like a drop of Scotch at Christmas.' Nan poured a larger measure into her tea and sat down.

'Bourbon, I should say,' she said, correcting herself. 'It's not Scotch. He would always pull me up on that. I bought him a bottle of Scotch once and it was no good. It had to be bourbon from Kentucky.'

Mr Rossi's two men arrived. When they knocked on the front door, Nan opened the dining room window and sent them around the back.

The older, fatter man appeared to be in charge. 'I'm sorry for your loss, Mrs Gallagher,' he said incorrectly.

'It's Callaghan, love,' Nan said, 'but it doesn't matter. He's over there.'

The younger, slimmer man had bad teeth. He copied everything his older colleague did and took instructions from him when they awkwardly bundled Grandad onto a stretcher and covered him up with a purple blanket.

Both men were dressed in smart black suits with white shirts and black ties, but they still managed to cut a shabby, unkempt appearance. I got the impression their sombre faces and polite words would break out into laughter and crass jokes the minute they were out of sight.

We stepped outside to watch them put Grandad in the back of their hearse and drive him away up Paynesdown Road.

After they had disappeared from view, we retreated inside and I felt a little lost, not knowing quite what to do with myself, and I suspected Nan felt the same when she announced an early lunch of soup and toast.

We ate and washed up in silence. Nan's thoughts seemed to be elsewhere, and I wondered what memories occupied her mind.

Then, after we'd cleared the washing-up, she said, 'I'm going to make some phone calls, love, to let my brothers and sisters know what's happened.'

With nothing else to do, I drifted into the lounge to switch on the TV. Before I sat down, I stopped at the fireplace. A framed picture of my parents' wedding day stood in the middle of the mantelpiece, flanked either side by two silver candle sticks with red unlit candles.

The photo had faded in the sunlight and my mother's white dress had been reduced to a watery shade of pale yellow, but the image was clear enough to see the features of their faces as they posed in the arched entrance of the church.

Their carefree smiles told me they knew nothing of what lay ahead.

I had been born eighteen months after their wedding and two years later they had died in a car crash. I had no clear memories of them.

Over my shoulder from the hallway door, I heard Nan say, 'Do you want to talk about them, love?'

My stomach churned and I looked sharply away from the photo.

'You've got to someday,' she added.

'No, I don't want to, not today,' I said.

I put the photo back on the mantlepiece, and when I turned, she greeted me with a hopeful expression.

'Alright, love, when you're ready,' she said, and she returned to the hall.

I switched on the TV and flicked through the channels, but when I couldn't find anything to watch, I went up to my room.

2

Nan kept herself busy that first weekend without Grandad.

We spent Saturday together. We caught the bus into Newbury to do the weekly shop in the morning and then curled up in front of the TV in the afternoon. Nan wanted to watch an old black-and-white film about a murder on a train and after that had finished, she made a start on dinner while I watched the football scores come in.

'How did your team get on?' she asked from the door.

'Lost one-nil.'

'Oh dear,' she said, 'your Aunty Florence won't be happy.'

After dinner, we switched between the channels until the boxing came on. By that time, I was ready for bed, but we'd decided when Grandad had died that we should stay up and watch it.

I had followed the build-up to the fight through the week in the newspapers, so I did have a mild interest in the outcome. The last fight between the two boxers had ended with a split decision and, according to the loser and some of the experts on TV, there had been some controversy with the scoring from the judges.

After trading insults on the back pages of the tabloids, scuffles broke out during the weigh-in and even the boxer's girlfriends had piled into the melee.

'The weigh-ins are more entertaining than the actual bloody fights these days,' Grandad had moaned on numerous occasions previously, and that proved to be the case once again.

The fight was stopped tamely at the end of the fifth round when the doctor stepped in. The boxer from Liverpool, who'd also lost the first fight, had a cut above his eye and he couldn't go on. Needless to say, he didn't agree with the decision. He harangued the doctor and his petite, half-naked girlfriend with big hair climbed into the ring to join him.

A wall of security guards had to circle the medical team and escort them from the arena, with the girlfriend swinging more punches than her middleweight boxer boyfriend.

'They should have sent her in earlier,' Nan said over her knitting. 'She's a better fighter than her fella.'

When they came back from the advert break and the panel of experts gave their opinions, the armchair next to me felt very empty.

'Do you think Grandad would have enjoyed it?' I asked Nan, while trying to imagine him sat there.

'Probably not, love,' she said. 'Come on, it's time for bed.'

On Sunday morning, Nan woke me to say she'd be out until late, but there were plenty of leftovers in the fridge for me to pick through.

She'd taken on some extra hours at The White Hart.

She did her usual cleaning shift in the morning and then stayed on to work behind the bar after they opened.

'Then after work, me and Marjorie are going straight to bingo,' she said.

On Monday morning, I went to school and left Nan alone in the house for the first time without Grandad.

She said, 'I'm fine, I really don't know what you're fussing about,' as I left but, even so, I decided to skip football practice after school and hurry straight back.

When I got home, I found the kitchen thick with steam and the smell of stew.

'Hello, love,' Nan said as she peeled potatoes. 'How was school?'

'Fine, thanks.'

Before I'd taken my coat off, she followed up with, 'Have you seen Freya lately?' And I got the impression she'd been sitting on the question for some time.

I had just finished a geography lesson with Freya. She sat in the first row of desks, opposite the teacher in the front corner of the classroom, and from my position up against the wall on the far side of the room, I'd spent the class, as I usually did, staring at the side of her face while the teacher, Miss Duxbury, had been speaking.

Freya had a habit of holding her pen up against her small, upturned nose as she pondered a problem, and when the teacher asked a question she knew the answer to, her knee would rapidly bounce up and down and she'd tuck her brown, bobbed hair behind her ear.

'Come on, one of you must know?' Miss Duxbury would say after asking the question again, but neither Freya nor I would ever put a hand up to answer.

'Well, have you?' Nan asked again. 'Have you seen Freya?'

'No, I don't think so,' I said dismissively. 'I don't really pay much attention.'

'Oh, alright then,' Nan said, clearly disappointed with my reply, 'but you must let me know if she says anything?'

'Why? Have you had another argument with her dad?'

She filled a saucepan and put it on the hob.

'No, no, it's nothing like that,' she said.

'Are you worried because Grandad's not here anymore?'

'No, don't be silly. But you know very well my feelings about that man.'

'But you've never told me why you don't like him. I know you've had lots of arguments, but you've never explained why.'

'It doesn't matter what's happened in the past, all that matters is that you keep your distance, alright?'

'You take her meals sometimes, don't you?' I asked. 'I've seen you go over there when Vic's not in.'

'Sometimes I do,' she said.

'Why? Doesn't Vic feed her properly?'

'Some men shouldn't be fathers,' she said, and she glanced up to read the expression on my face.

'Does he hurt her?'

'No, love,' Nan said. 'Not that I know of, at least not physically.'

'But she's scared of him, isn't she?'

'Yes, love. A lot of people are scared of him.'

'And that's why Larry only sees Freya secretly?'

'Yes, he sees her when he can.'

'And Larry's her uncle?'

'No, he's her godfather; Larry and her mum were very close.'

'Why don't we—'

'I've told you,' Nan interrupted, 'to stay well clear of him, and that's what you're going to do.'

'Alright,' I agreed, but I wasn't ready to let it pass. 'So why did you ask about Freya? What do you expect her to say?'

'It doesn't matter. I just feel for the poor girl, that's all. So, you keep an eye out for her, and you let me know if you hear anything.'

I made a pot of tea and sat down at the dining room table with the newspaper. I skimmed through the sports news, but my mind strayed back to Freya and her dad, Vic Dyson.

'When did Freya's mum die?' I asked, turning the page.

Nan swung around from the cooker. She seemed annoyed I hadn't let it drop, but she answered anyway. 'It must be a good seven or eight years ago now. Do you remember anything about it? I'm not sure you were old enough.'

'I'm not sure, maybe,' I said as I thought back.

I did have a hazy memory of Nan wearing a black hat and a black coat with a fur trim. Her heels clicked on the kitchen floor tiles as she paced up and down and the word 'funeral' hung in the air.

From the lounge, I watched her pointing through the arch as she spoke to Grandad in the dining room. Although I couldn't see Grandad, I could hear him well enough and the phrase, 'there's nothing you can do, there's nothing you can do', came back to me.

The conversation became quite heated, but it didn't feel like one of their arguments and, for some reason, I couldn't remember anything Nan had said. When she saw me listening in, she came into the lounge. I remember she spoke to me in a comforting tone, but her words escaped me and the memory ends with her closing the door.

'How did she die?' I asked.

'There was an accident,' Nan said vaguely, 'the poor woman, it was an absolute tragedy.'

'But how did she die? What sort of accident was it?'

'She fell.'

'Really?'

'Yes. She fell and caught her head, and she died from it. Just like that, she was dead and poor Freya was left alone with that bastard.'

She placed a second saucepan on the hob and turned on the gas.

'Keep an eye on these, will you?' she said. 'Turn them down when they start to boil over. I'm just going round Shirley's to borrow some flour.'

She slipped out the back door.

Ever since Grandad's death, I had carried around a feeling that we had come to the end of something. But now, alone and waiting for the pots and pans to boil over as the gas rings roared, that feeling left me.

3

When I returned home from school on Thursday, I found Nan in the kitchen with her coat and shoes on. To keep the weather out, she'd wrapped her blue-and-purple floral headscarf around the top of her head and tied it off with a bow under her chin.

She adjusted the bow in the kitchen mirror and said, 'I'm looking after Sita's kids for a bit while she goes out.'

'Alright,' I said. 'What time will you be back?'

'Not sure. It could be late. There's some cottage pie in the oven for you and I made some bread pudding as well, it's over there. Oh, and Larry called. He wants you to go round there a week on Sunday to help out in the garden. He said he'd pay you.'

'OK,' I said, looking out the dining room window. 'Who are those men outside? Have they come to cut the trees down?'

'No, love. They are from the Council, but they're planning to paint all the houses.'

'That's good, I thought for a minute they'd changed their minds about the trees.'

'No, love,' she said, pulling the door open. 'They wrote last week to say they'd come round and take a look before they started work. Right, I'm off. I'll see you later.'

Two years before, the Council had sent a letter informing us the conifer trees running down the side of our garden had to be cut down. They claimed the roots had started to lift the pavement and were causing a hazard. Nan didn't take it well. Within minutes of receiving the letter, she'd dragged me from my breakfast to inspect the path outside.

'There's nothing wrong with it,' she said angrily, tapping the sole of her slipper down on the bulges in the tarmac where the tree roots had raised it. She stormed back inside and said, 'There is no way I'll let them cut those trees down.'

Families of blackbirds had nested in the conifers ever since Nan and Grandad had moved in and to encourage them, Nan had bought a birdbath and a bird table and positioned them in the corner of the garden. In winter, she would make sure they had plenty of food and water and in summer she enjoyed sitting outside to watch them fuss and flutter to and fro.

When she wrote to the Council, she argued the pavement hadn't been disturbed and the roads and paths elsewhere on the estate were in a far worse condition. 'They're only doing it so they can save a few quid trimming them back each year,' she fumed, and her letter went on to say as much.

She included photos of the path outside and other parts of the estate to support her argument.

After receiving a second letter from the Council confirming the work had to happen, Nan went to their offices and had a big bust–up with some of the Council staff there.

'I lost my temper, Jamie,' she confided to me at dinnertime that night and I had visions of grown men in suits running for cover in the Council offices while this tiny old lady went on the rampage, screaming and shouting at them.

Nevertheless, the Council insisted the trees had to come down, and they followed up with yet another letter confirming the date it would happen. This time the letter had been written by a lawyer and included lots of legal clauses and jargon we couldn't understand.

Nan wouldn't back down. She spoke to the neighbours, and they all agreed to park their cars and block the workmen when they arrived. Somebody even called the Newbury Weekly News, who promised to send out a reporter on the day to cover the protest.

I began to worry. I didn't want the trees cut down, but, more importantly, I didn't want Nan to get into trouble with lawyers and people like that.

Thankfully, we had a stroke of good fortune.

To pay off a vet's bill for one of Ollie's operations, Nan had worked a few extra shifts on Saturday nights at The White Hart. On one of those nights, she struck up a conversation about the conifers with a group of Saturday-night regulars and, as it turned out, one of them worked for a company the Council used to produce environmental reports. He thought he might be able to help.

Nan reportedly told him, 'There's a good drink in it for you,' but he said he'd be happy to help for nothing and he didn't want any money.

The following Sunday morning, we woke to find him rummaging around in our conifers with a notebook and pen and a Polaroid camera hanging from a strap around his neck.

From the kitchen window, Nan said to me, 'He's a doctor, you know, but not your normal doctor type of doctor.'

He certainly didn't look like any doctor I'd seen before with his khaki fisherman's hat and thick bushy grey moustache. When he bent over in the bushes, his trousers slipped and we could see most of his excessively hairy backside. 'Ugh,' Nan said, as she pulled a face and moved away from the window.

When he came inside, I suspected he was drunk. He bumped into the cooker and the kitchen cupboards and his eyes lit up when Nan offered him a drink, only to fall back crestfallen when she asked, 'Tea or coffee?'

We all gathered around the dining room table (even Grandad was keen to join us) and Doctor Eric, which is what everybody called him, took us through a pack of photographs of caterpillars crawling over conifer branches. I asked him if the pictures were really taken from our garden, and when he smiled and said, 'Of course they are, Jamie,' I knew they definitely weren't.

He said he'd write a report to the Council, telling them they couldn't tear down the trees because the rare caterpillars breeding there had to be protected. He did as well. He sent the report and, to everybody's amazement, it worked. A week later, we received a single-line letter from the Council informing us the work had been cancelled due to unforeseen circumstances.

After the long, drawn-out battle we'd had with the Council, I must admit my surprise at Nan's muted celebrations. When I returned home from school, Nan simply handed me the letter without a word and left me to read it alone. But after dinner, we did move some dining room chairs outside to spend the evening at the bottom of the garden, watching the blackbirds dart in and out of their nests up in the trees.

Grandad kept on saying, time and time again, 'It's not what you know, it's who you know,' while I fed the birds bits of bread torn from a stale loaf. After Grandad had repeated it for the fifth or sixth time, I thought Nan would tell him to shut up, but she didn't.

She just sat there quietly smoking and when she did speak, she said, 'Jamie, make sure that little one over there gets some bread.'

With Nan on her way to Sita's flat and the conifer trees on my mind, I let the dogs out and followed after them.

There was a position in the conifers, past the blackbird's nests and close to the fence at the back of the garden, where I could climb inside between the branches, sit comfortably enough, and see out across the street.

From there, hidden among the trees, I would sometimes catch a glimpse of Freya either returning home late from school or trying to shoot a basket in the netball hoop in her back yard. I knew my chances of seeing her were slim at this time of year, but even so, I waited and I hoped.

The first streetlamp had flickered on in the fading light and a flurry of cars with people heading home from work had passed when I heard men's voices and laughter at the rear of Freya's house.

The garage obscured my view and, at first, I thought the voices must be the men from the Council, but I was soon proven wrong.

Freya's dad, Vic Dyson, emerged from behind his garage, and his long lazy stride brought him across the road towards our side gate.

He wore scruffy jeans and a tight-fitting white tee shirt that stretched across his bulging stomach and he had something in his hand I couldn't quite see. More laughter broke out from the men hidden behind the garage when he swivelled his head back towards them and grinned.

As he drew closer to our gate, he held out whatever it was he was holding, and from my position tucked inside the conifers at the far end of our garden, I lost sight of him.

The three men with Vic were still laughing when they came into view. Two of them had skinheads, and they wore skinny jeans with big, heavy boots. They looked like brothers, with the taller, bigger-built one rocking on the balls of his feet with his hands in his pockets. The other brother leant forward on Vic's garden fence, and his denim jacket gaped open to expose a crumpled red teeshirt with what looked like a white circle and some type of black markings.

A third-fatter, balding man wearing a charcoal-grey business suit with a half-untucked cream shirt and a purple tie loosened around his neck came up behind them. He moved slowly, with an air of authority, and when he stopped and folded his arms, he made a quip the two brothers were quick to laugh at.

Stan and Ollie ran over to the gate. Whatever Vic held in his hand had drawn the dogs to him.

An uneasy feeling came over me and the next sound I heard sent a surge of panic coursing through my chest. One of the dogs squealed in pain. Vic had grabbed hold of it. I'd been determined to stay put and out of sight, but I knew in an instant I could no longer stay hidden.

A stray branch scratched my left cheek as I hurriedly scrambled out from inside the trees. I felt my face for blood as I shifted forward, but none had been drawn. When I reached the gate, I found Vic cradling Ollie, one arm underneath with the other hand holding the back of his neck.

Stan repeatedly jumped up at the fence, his delirious snarling bark wild and without rhythm.

Ollie screeched in pain a second time.

I rushed forward and said, 'Give me my dog back.'

Vic glared at me. His close-cropped black hair ran into his dark unshaven stubble and his expressionless face had a yellowish, unwashed tinge to it.

I said, 'You're hurting him,' and my voice cracked as I said it.

Vic refused to speak and something in his black eyes gave me the impression he could erupt into violence at any moment.

The three men watched from across the road. When the balding man in the suit unfolded his arms and strolled across the street, a keychain dangling from his belt with a dozen or so keys knocked against his leg as he strode forward. He turned and uttered something to the other two, and the taller brother snorted a laugh.

Ollie yelped as the grip around his neck tightened and Vic's blank expression turned to one of pleasure as he watched me suffer.

I held the top of our wooden gate with both hands and said to Vic, 'Please give him back, you're hurting him. Why are you hurting him?'

'I'm not hurting him,' he said at last, 'but he should be put down. He's old and sick and he's got a bad eye. Look.'

'He's fine. Just give him to me and he'll be fine.'

Stan hadn't stopped barking, but he now started to tire. He ran to my ankles and yapped at me.

A tear ran down my face and fell from my chin. 'Please stop,' I shouted desperately.

'Hello, Jamie,' the balding man said as he arrived and stood alongside Vic. 'We thought we saw you hiding over there in the trees.'

'He's hurting my dog,' I said.

'Look at this, Ted,' Vic said, as he held Ollie up. 'He should be put down.'

'Yep, looks like it,' Ted agreed, before saying to me, 'I'm sorry to hear your grandad's dead, Jamie. Sad news, that. So, it's just the two of you now then, just you and your gran. I wonder where you will go when something happens to her?'

'What?' I said. 'I don't know, just give me my dog back.'

'But he should be put down,' Vic said, raising his voice.

Ted nodded. 'We can take care of it for you, Jamie.'

'No. Stop hurting him, and he'll be fine.'

'But, Jamie, you don't need to worry. We can take care of it for you. We can get the dog put down. It's for the best.'

'No. No, give him back.'

'What's that?' Ted said. 'You want us to give him back? You want us to give him back and go away? You don't want us to interfere?'

'No,' I said again, and I sniffed and wiped my wet face with the back of my hand.

'Alright, Jamie,' Ted said, 'why didn't you say so. If you don't want us to interfere, we won't. It's not very nice when people interfere, is it?' He leaned in towards me and the tone in his voice changed. 'Just make sure your gran knows not to interfere, OK? Your grandad's not here to look after her anymore, is he? We can come over and say "hello" anytime we want to now, can't we?'

'We know what she's planning,' Ted went on, 'but nothing will change around here. They won't reopen the case against Vic when I retire. You tell her that from me, and you make sure she doesn't try anything.'

Vic carelessly dropped Ollie over the fence, and he landed awkwardly on his side. I crouched down, scooped Ollie into my arms, and held him close to my chest as I faced away from the men. Stan yapped at the fence, and I heard footsteps recede as they walked across the street, and then more laughter when they gathered together.

With Ollie in my arms, I hurried in the back door. Stan followed, and I closed the door and turned the key to lock it.

I perched on a dining room chair and held Ollie for a few minutes and when his breathing slowed, I took him to the corner of the kitchen. He lapped at his water bowl before settling in his basket and Stan climbed in with him.

I moved a chair from the dining room table to the window, and I pulled the curtain to leave a slender gap, so I could see if Vic or the others came back.

As I sat there staring out at the empty street, I replayed over every word they had said to me. None of it made any sense. I knew Nan had fallen out with Vic, but I'd assumed they'd argued about one of them parking a car in the wrong place or making too much noise; the usual things neighbours would argue about. It was clear to me now there was far more to it, but what? I couldn't understand what they meant when they said, 'we know what she's planning,' and 'you make sure she doesn't try anything.' What could she possibly be planning?

The first few spots of rain fell. The first shower lasted several minutes but the rain grew steadily heavier, and dirt-brown puddles formed in the uneven recesses of the road.

After 25 minutes, the three men left Vic's house. The two brothers climbed into Ted's blue car and they drove away.

Nobody else passed by for over an hour before Nan eventually came into view, walking down Paynesdown Road from the bus stop. She angled her black umbrella towards the rain and dragged her tartan shopping bag on wheels behind her.

I unlocked the door and greeted her as she closed her umbrella and shook off the worst of the water outside.

I blurted out, 'Vic came here with some men.'

She had begun to peel off her coat, but she stopped with it half off. 'What did you say?'

'Vic came here. There were some men with him. He had Ollie and wouldn't give him back.'

'Jamie, slow down. They came in here?'

'No, they were outside the gate, but Vic picked up Ollie.'

Nan looked past me at the dogs sleeping in their basket.

'But Ollie's OK?'

'Vic hurt him; he squeezed his neck but he's alright now.'

'They didn't hurt you, did they?'

'No, they didn't touch me.'

'How many of them were there?'

'Four.'

'What did they look like?' she asked, removing her coat and hanging it up.

'There was a fat one called Ted and two others who stayed over the road. They were skinny and looked like brothers and they had shaved heads.'

Nan went into the dining room and lowered herself carefully into her chair.

She didn't look at me and with eyes fixed on the window, she asked, 'What else did they say, Jamie? I need to know everything.'

'They said they know you're planning something. They kept saying, "don't interfere."'

'What else?' she asked. 'They must have said something else?' She dragged the ashtray across the table and put a cigarette in her mouth, but she didn't light it.

'I don't know. They said lots of things, but they had Ollie.' I thought it over some more before saying, 'They said they could come here and say "hello" any time they wanted now Grandad was gone, and they asked where I would go when you were gone, and the fat one said something about nothing changing when he retires.'

'Jamie, Jamie, calm down. Don't worry.' She forced a smile. 'It's a misunderstanding. It's nothing more than that and it's nothing to worry about. I'll straighten it out. OK?'

'But what's it all about? What are you planning?'

'Nothing. Really, it's nothing to worry about. Alright?'

She reached out a hand and placed it on mine to reassure me. 'Trust me, everything will be alright.'

'OK,' I said reluctantly.

'I do have some good news,' she said, gently squeezing my hand.

'But—'

'Jamie,' she interrupted. 'Everything will be alright; I promise, and you need to listen because I've got some good news. Your Aunty Flo is coming to live with us. Not just to stay for a bit, but to live here permanently.'

'Really?'

'She's already sold her caravan in Hayling Island and she's moving up here next Saturday. It makes sense now Grandad isn't here. I knew you'd be pleased.'

'I am pleased,' I said. 'It's good you won't be alone when I'm at school.'

'Enough,' she snapped. 'I'll be fine with or without your Aunty Florence being here. You mustn't worry. It's all just a misunderstanding and I'll sort it out. I don't want to hear any more of it. Alright? Now go and make us some tea.'

When I returned with the tea, I tried for a second time to find out what was going on, but Nan refused to speak of it. We sat quietly before Nan made her excuses and slipped away to call Aunty Flo and I went through to the lounge to watch TV. I returned for Ollie, picking him up out of his basket and putting him on my lap. Stan followed and jumped up onto the settee.

The snooker had started but I struggled to focus on it, my mind constantly reliving what had happened. Stan nestled in closer to my leg and he extended a paw to rest it on Ollie's back.

'Don't worry, Ollie,' I whispered in his ear as he slept, 'Aunty Flo's coming. She'll help us.'

4

On Friday night after dinner, I had hoped to settle down in front of the TV, but instead, Nan sent me up to the attic.

The ladder unfolded onto our landing at the top of the stairs and I climbed up.

A water tank dripped in the corner and although warm air filtered up through the opening in the ceiling, it did little to ease the biting cold.

Nan followed me up the ladder but stopped part way with the hatch up to her waist.

'It's down there,' she said, pointing into the darkness, down into the long, unfamiliar end of the loft on the opposite side to where we kept the Christmas decorations.

I asked, 'Are you sure there isn't a light?'

'No, love,' she replied. 'But I've got this.'

Nan clicked on a black plastic torch and beamed a shaft of light past me to the end of the attic. Through the timber roof trusses and past a scattering of half-filled cardboard boxes and plastic containers, the torch rested on a mound of objects in the far corner, cloaked in a grubby white sheet.

'Take this,' Nan said, 'and make sure you only walk on these.'

She gave me the torch and tapped one of the wooden joists running the width of the loft.

'Whatever you do, don't tread on this stuff or you'll go through the bloody ceiling,' she said, referring to the pink fluffy insulation that filled the gaps in between the joists.

'Go on,' Nan said, 'get going.'

Holding on to a rafter and crouching over slightly with the pitch of the roof, I took my first step over an old lampshade tipped on its side and I shuffled forward.

Some of the pink insulation stuck to my sock as I stepped across the joists.

'Don't touch that stuff, try to brush it off with something,' Nan said, so I stopped to scrape it off against a rafter before moving on.

As I drew closer to the end of the loft, I directed the torch beam over to the white sheet, but it was impossible to tell what lay hidden beneath it.

I grabbed hold of the next stanchion and cautiously stepped onto the cork floorboards set out to support whatever it was I'd been sent up to collect.

'Are you there yet, love?' Nan called. 'What have you found?'

'I'm here,' I shouted back. 'I'm just about to take a look.'

A cloud of dust billowed up when I pulled the sheet away. I stepped back and stooped down to get away from the worst of it, but it stung my eyes and stuck in my throat as I breathed in.

'Are you alright, love?' Nan asked when she heard me choking.

'Yeah, I'm fine,' I managed to shout back. 'It's just a bit dusty.'

I rubbed my eyes and searched through the dust, and the light from the torch revealed black bin bags of old clothes and numerous cardboard boxes of differing sizes, all piled up around a battered red suitcase lying flat on its side.

The three largest boxes were open at the top. I found the first stuffed with vinyl records and the remaining two filled with an old crockery set of china bowls and plates and cups in a brown-and-orange pattern.

I wiped a layer of grimy dust from another two smaller boxes to reveal yellow stickers with labels written in what appeared to be Nan's handwriting. The boxes were taped shut and the labels read:

"Letters: 1944" and "Letters: 1945–46".

'What have you found, love?'

'I've found bags of clothes, a suitcase and some cardboard boxes,' I yelled back. 'There are some plates and bowls, a box with records, and some small boxes with letters in.'

'That's them,' she said. 'Bring the letters back with you.'

The sound of the phone ringing carried up into the attic as I picked up the two boxes of letters.

'Hold on, love,' Nan said. 'Let me go and get that.'

By the time I'd returned to the loft hatch, Nan was shouting up the stairs.

'Jamie, that was Sita. They've had a fire, so I'm going round to see if I can help.'

'A fire?' I bellowed. 'Is everyone alright? Do you want me to come with you?'

'Everyone's safe, love, but they're in a bit of a state. You stay here and I'll be back as soon as I can.'

The door slammed as she left. I moved to climb down but paused with one foot on the ladder, and then changed my mind and hauled myself back up.

Leaving the boxes of letters at the top of the ladder, I picked up the torch and returned to the red suitcase.

In near darkness, I shifted the heavy box of records. For a moment, I thought the bottom would give out, but I managed to keep it intact and heave it off the suitcase. I knelt down at the case and pressed the two metal latches to release the lid. When I opened it up, I found the case overflowing with a heap of photographs of differing shapes and sizes.

Most of the photos were in colour and appeared to have been taken quite recently, but there were a smattering of older, black-and-white pictures with clothes and cars and hairstyles from a different time.

I thought it strange there were pictures of Nan, Grandad and me together with aunties, uncles and cousins, but none of my parents.

Close to the top of the pile, I stuck on a photo Nan had taken of me, stood grinning on a beach in swimming trunks next to an ill-tempered Grandad. He wore his white sleeveless vest with braces pinned to his chest and full-length trousers. He sat hunched over awkwardly in a blue-and-white striped deck chair.

With the photo and the torch, I sat down to rest against a wooden truss.

I heard a car swoosh past and the murmur of voices outside and the memory of that day on the beach swirled in my mind. We were on holiday in Devon, and I had just come out of the sea, with my castle-shaped bucket full of sea water. I remembered how the plastic handle of the bucket felt strapped across my fingers when I carried it up the crowded beach from the water's edge.

'God, it's hot,' I could hear Grandad say, mopping at his brow with a handkerchief and glaring in disgust at the young couple lying on a towel next to us as they kissed and giggled.

Thunderstorms had been forecast but the weather had held, and we spent the day on the beach until late afternoon, when we headed back to the caravan. I lagged a few paces behind Nan and Grandad as we walked along the seafront.

'I'll make us some sandwiches,' Nan had said to Grandad, 'and then you two can get away. Don't forget you're driving Jamie up to the football tonight.'

'We're doing what?' Grandad said gruffly.

'You're taking Jamie to football. His team are playing a friendly up at Exeter, so you said you'd take him. It's tonight. Remember?'

'No, no, I don't know anything about it.'

'Yes, you do. Bill, we agreed it all weeks ago. It's tonight. I reminded you at breakfast this morning. Jamie's been looking forward to it.'

Grandad hadn't stopped shaking his head. 'No, I can't do it,' he said. 'I can't go out tonight.'

'What do you mean, you can't do it?' Nan stopped and put her bags down. 'Of course you can. You promised him you would. It's why we came down this weekend.'

Grandad had walked on, but he now stopped and turned. He blinked repeatedly and continued to shake his head. 'I can't do it,' he said angrily. 'I can't. I've got to take my tablets.'

Nan raised her voice. 'Just take them when you get there.'

'No, I can't.'

'Why not?' Nan shouted. 'You take them when we're out all the time.'

A married couple walked past with their two daughters. One of the girls looked older, but her sister appeared to be the same age as me. The parents and the older daughter were embarrassed by the argument, and they gazed out to sea to avoid eye contact, but the younger girl grinned at me and the moment we crossed, she erupted into laughter.

'You take him,' Grandad shot back. 'Why can't you take him?'

'But you need to drive him. It's the other side of Exeter. We can't get back if we take the bus. I've told you all of this.'

'No, I can't do it. I'm not doing it.'

'Now you listen to me.' Nan stepped forward, pointing her finger. 'You promised him. It's his football team.'

Grandad grabbed at Nan's wrist and her frail hand shook like a wilting flower in the wind.

'It's his dad's fucking team,' he snarled. 'Regan should be taking him.'

'But Regan's not here,' Nan screamed. 'Regan's gone, it's just us. It's just us left to look after him.'

People on the beach were staring now.

'You think I don't know he's gone?' Grandad shouted. 'He's gone and he's never coming back. Now will you listen to me? I'm not fucking doing it. I need my tablets.' Grandad threw down her arm and stormed away.

Nan gathered up her bags and delayed as long as she reasonably could before facing me with an apologetic smile. 'I'm sorry about the football, Jamie,' she said. 'I know you were looking forward to it.'

'That's alright, don't worry,' I said, and we slowly walked back.

By the time we returned to the caravan, Grandad had shut himself away in the bedroom and we didn't see him for the rest of the day. After Nan and I had both taken showers to rinse off the sand from the beach, we drank tea and watched the portable TV in the caravan.

When Nan's soaps had finished, she said, 'Let's go out and get some supper.'

We ambled into town as the lights along the promenade switched on and we bought fish and chips in an old-fashioned shop opposite a pub with tables and hanging flowers outside. The forecast rain arrived as we unwrapped the chip paper, so we moved from our bench overlooking the beach to take shelter in a covered bus stop. I tried to think of things to say while Nan waved the buses on when they stopped to pick us up. The rain continued steadily and after we'd finished eating, we walked home together huddled under her umbrella.

We went to bed early, but I couldn't sleep, lying awake for hours. The rain had turned into a storm with the wind shaking the caravan and the pelting noise of rain beating down on the lightweight roof.

When the door of my bedroom opened, I couldn't see for the dark, but I knew from the rhythm of the footsteps it was Grandad.

'Jamie, Jamie, wake up,' he said, giving me a nudge.

'Come and watch the fight with me. Our man just won the first round. We've got the Yank on the run.'

I followed in my pyjamas and he turned with his finger to his lips. 'Shhh, keep the noise down,' he whispered, 'your nan's asleep.'

He adjusted the volume on the TV, and then ushered me into the seat by the window.

The TV burst into life. A punch landed and the commentator screeched out in excitement.

One of the boxers fell back into the ropes. I didn't know who was who, but I guessed the American had just been hit from the tone of the partisan commentary team. After bouncing off the ropes, he grabbed hold of the other boxer and held him in a bear hug while the puny referee with white hair tried to prise them apart.

'He's got him again, Jamie, he's got him again.' Grandad ruffled my hair and squeezed into the seat next to me. Reaching over, he picked up a mug from the table and thrust it into my hand. 'I made you a hot chocolate,' he said.

A cloudburst of rain lashed down on the caravan and the TV crackled.

I sipped my drink and watched Grandad's face in the flickering light of the screen as the Englishman led with two left jabs and followed with a right.

'Look, the Yank can't even see his right cross coming,' he said with relish. 'He's just too fast for him, Jamie, he's just too fast.'

5

Nan didn't return until after midnight.

I'd spent most of the evening in the loft sifting through the photos in the suitcase, before taking the boxes of Grandad's letters down to Nan's room and then finally settling in the warmth of the lounge to watch television.

An American comedy show had just finished when I heard Nan at the door. I turned the TV off and went through to the kitchen.

'Hello, love,' she said, taking off her coat. 'Put the kettle on, will you?'

'Is Sita alright?' I asked.

The dogs had rushed to greet Nan at the back door. She crouched down to stroke them, but not with the same vigour she usually had. 'Have you let these two out for the night?'

'Yes, they've already been out. Nan, are Sita and her family alright?'

'Nobody's hurt, love,' she said, slowly rising to her feet, 'but there's an awful lot of damage. Make me a cup of tea and I'll tell you; I just need to spend a penny first. Oh, and I've run out of fags. Will you fetch me the packet from in there?'

'Nan, are you OK?' I asked.

'Yes, love, I'm fine. I'm just a bit tired, that's all.'

I made tea and collected Nan's cigarettes from the lounge. When she came downstairs, we sat across from each other at the dining room table and she explained what had happened.

'They reckon their dry cleaners will be shut for months and there's an awful lot a smoke damage upstairs in their flat too. They've had to move out and it could be weeks before they can get back in.'

Her words came quickly, as if she had a lot to say but wanted to get it over and done with.

'Where have they gone?' I asked.

'I said they could come here, but Rahul wasn't keen, so they've got a hotel in Newbury. Their insurance people have set it all up for them and told them not to worry about the cost of it.'

Nan lit a cigarette and after a long drag, she balanced it on the edge of the ashtray so she could cup her mug of tea with both hands.

'That's where I've been,' she went on, 'at the hotel. Rahul took me and the kids there and then went back to help Sita clear up what they could while I put the children to bed. The poor little things were terrified.'

'How did the fire start?' I asked.

'Not sure,' Nan replied. 'There were still firemen and an investigator looking around when I first got there, so I guess they'll try to work it out. One of the firemen told me that most fires are caused by electrical faults, so they reckon it could have been one of the driers.'

'At least they all got out and nobody was hurt.'

'Well, that's the thing,' she said, holding her mug up before taking a sip. 'It's a bloody disaster but they were lucky really. Their fire alarm packed up a couple of weeks ago and they only had it repaired on Wednesday. I hate to think what would have happened without it. Sita had put the kids to bed, and they were having their dinner when they heard the alarm go off downstairs. At first, they thought it was a false alarm. Rahul went downstairs thinking something else had set it off, but by the time he got there, the whole of the downstairs was ablaze. He went back up to get Sita and the kids out and they didn't even have time to phone 999. Luckily, Jackie, over at The White Hart, saw the flames through the window and she phoned the fire brigade, who were there in no time. That's the frightening thing, love. It could've been so much worse than it was.'

She sat forward to say something else, but at the last moment she checked and thought better of it. I noticed the slightest of frowns as she drew on her cigarette, as if she was chastising herself for what she had almost said.

I felt the need to speak. 'I'm just glad that everyone's alright.'

'Yes, me too, love.' She glanced over at the clock and stretched out her arms. Stifling a yawn, she said, 'Right, come on, we need to get you up to bed. Leave these cups. I'll do them in the morning.'

Sita called in to see us the following day. She knocked on the back door before letting herself in, so I knew it was her. Nobody else ever bothered to knock.

Her eyes were swollen and the smeared tracks of tears were still evident on her cheeks even though she'd tried to wipe them away.

Nan met her with a hug. Sita's face creased with emotion when they embraced, and I thought she might cry again.

'I'll make us all a cup of tea,' I said, pretending not to notice.

Sita handed Nan a carrier bag. 'Rahul told me to buy you flowers but I thought you'd prefer these. Thank you so much for your help yesterday.'

'Oh, Sita,' Nan said, peering into the bag. 'There was no need. Really, you didn't need to get me anything.'

'Yes, I did, Betty, and I owe you for so much more, not just yesterday, but for everything else you've done for us. If there is ever anything I can do for you, anything at all, you must ask me.'

'You don't owe me anything, Sita, but thank you for these.' Nan gave me the carrier bag, filled with a box of 200 cigarettes, and said, 'Put these in the cupboard and put the kettle on, love.'

Over tea at the dining room table, Sita told us the investigation into the fire was ongoing and she went on to explain the argument she'd had with Rahul that morning. She didn't like the hotel they were in, and the insurance company had advised it could take up to six weeks to get them back into their flat.

'You're all welcome to come here,' Nan said. 'It's much closer to the kid's school and we've got the spare room you could have. We'd love to have you here, wouldn't we, Jamie?'

'Yes, of course,' I agreed.

'No, Betty, that's very kind of you, but Rahul would never agree to it.' Sita's eyes reddened. Holding back tears, she said to me, 'When I get back home, Jamie, I will cook you one of my special meals and bring it round. I'm sorry I've not made you anything for such a long time, but I promise I will make it up to you. Your nan always tells me how much you love my cooking.'

'Yes please,' I said, 'that would be great, thanks.'

'Jamie would love that,' Nan said, 'but I've been meaning to talk to you about something, Sita. Jamie, you'd better go and feed the dogs, love, they must be starving.'

I checked the clock. It wasn't quite time for the dogs to eat yet, but I left them together at the table and did as she asked.

From the kitchen, I strained to overhear what Nan had to say. Reaching for a can of dog food at the back of the cupboard, I heard Nan's hushed voice. 'I understand you've been cooking meals and taking them across the road. Why have you been doing that? I've told you, Sita, you've got to stay well clear of him.'

'Oh, Betty, I knew you wouldn't like it,' Sita replied, 'but Vic could make life very difficult for Rahul at the factory. We can't survive on the money from the dry cleaners alone, so he needs that job. I've made a few meals for some of Rahul's close friends there and when Vic heard about it, he asked Rahul if I would make something for him. I couldn't say no, could I? I've heard all the rumours, and I knew you wouldn't like it, but I had no choice.'

I ran the tin opener around the can of dog food and called through to Stan and Ollie, who scampered in from the lounge.

Nan continued to speak, but I couldn't make out what was being said over the noise the dogs made.

In an attempt to listen in on the rest of the exchange, I moved to the sink, topped up the dog's water bowl and pretended to wash something up. I picked out the occasional word, but I couldn't string enough together to get the gist of what was being said. By the time the dogs had finished eating, Sita had returned to the kitchen and the conversation had softened into pleasant goodbyes.

At the door, Nan forced an envelope into Sita's reluctant hand. I thought that Sita would burst into tears, but Nan said her final goodbye and quickly guided her out the door.

Nan leant on the door after she'd closed it. 'That poor woman,' she said with a sigh.

I searched for something to say, and ended up blurting out, 'Is she OK?'

'No, not really, love.'

'Did you give her our holiday money?'

'Yeah,' Nan replied. 'I know Rahul won't give her any of the insurance money, so she can get the kids something nice with it. You don't mind, do you?'

'No, of course not.'

'Thanks, love,' Nan said, as she collected the teacups from the dining room table.

When she put them in the sink, I asked her, 'Did you see I put the boxes in your room?'

She frowned. 'What?'

'The boxes with Grandad's letters, I put them under the window in your bedroom.'

'Yes, that's right,' she said. 'Thanks for doing that,

love. I'd completely forgotten all about them. You should go through them when you get a chance.'

'Why? What do they say?'

'Lots of things,' she said, 'and I think you might like them. They were all written before your grandad got sick, and I think you'll find them interesting.'

I washed up the teacups, then I went up to her room and crouched down by the boxes.

The tape on the box labelled "Letters: 1944" peeled back easily enough and when I opened out the lid, one of the dirty white envelopes, wedged in side by side, stood proud of the others. I pulled out the envelope, written to an address in London, and raised the one next to it to mark its place. I took it through to my room, and after curling up on my bed, I withdrew the letter from the envelope and unfolded three crumbled pages, each with writing crammed in on both sides.

Stan wandered in and jumped up onto the bed with me.

"Dear Betty," the letter began, in untidy handwriting scrawled in black ink.

6

SOMEWHERE IN BELGIUM, 1944

'But why us?' Callaghan asked. 'Why me and Baxter? Why do we have to go?'

'Don't for one minute think you were my first choice, Callaghan.' Captain Douglas-Sykes stood up straight, leaving the map in place on the table in front of him. 'Maynard and Hinchcliffe were dispatched at 0700 yesterday morning.'

Callaghan couldn't place Hinchcliffe, but he knew Maynard. A good-looking, confident guy from Yorkshire who knew his football. He seemed to remember a conversation with him one night not long after landing in Normandy. They spoke about athletics, and how Maynard specialised in sprinting and long jump and how he'd beaten some kind of record that hadn't been beaten for 30-odd years. He did agree with the captain on one thing, Maynard had been a good choice for this kind of thing.

Callaghan asked, 'But sir, even if they've met up with the Yanks, they wouldn't be back by now.'

'That's correct, Private.'

'So why do you need us to go?'

'I need that radio. It's as simple as that.' The captain took off his cap to reveal his perfectly coiffed blond hair and he eased his palm over it. 'The whole battalion has been at risk since ours went down. Believe me, risking two more privates to improve our chances of getting a live radio is not a difficult decision.'

Arguing was pointless, Callaghan knew that. He swivelled his head to watch a Jeep drive past the open side of the captain's field tent, before stepping closer to the table and motioning for Baxter to join him.

'So, we head due north,' Callaghan said, leaning on the map and running his finger across it. 'Cut across these fields to meet this road, and then follow the road northwest to where the Americans are, just south of that town.'

'That's right,' said the captain. 'Give or take, it's about 14 miles.'

Baxter spoke for the first time. 'Will they definitely be there, sir?' he asked anxiously.

'Based on the latest information we have, that's where they should be.'

'But what if they're not there, sir?'

'Then we've got to look for them,' Callaghan said to Baxter before addressing the captain again. 'So, if our radio is down, when did you get that information?'

The captain put his cap back on. 'You don't need to know that, Private.'

Callaghan shook his head, but he didn't speak. The captain pointed to another point on the map, in between their position and the Americans, but slightly to the west.

'There's something else you need to know; a retreating German battalion was last seen here moving east to join up with a division here.'

'Straight across our path?' Callaghan blurted out. 'So even though Maynard may already have the radio, you're still willing to send us out there?'

'Yes, I am.'

Callaghan laughed, shooting Baxter a look.

'I hate to break it to you, soldier,' the captain said, 'but compared to the rest of the battalion, your life is not that important to me.'

'Well, sir,' Callaghan said, as he met the captain's gaze and fought off the urge to blink, 'that does not surprise me in the slightest.'

The captain slammed his hand down on the table. 'Your mission, Private,' he shouted, 'is to obtain a spare radio from Major Turnbull. If he is not where we think he is, you go looking for him. If you encounter the enemy, you go around them. Whatever happens, you continue with the task in hand. Am I making myself clear?'

'Perfectly clear, sir,' said Callaghan.

'You leave in one hour. Jenkins will tell you the rest and give you provisions. Dismissed.'

Both privates stiffened to attention, saluted, and turned to leave.

'One more thing, Callaghan,' the captain said to their backs.

'Sir?'

'Unless it's already on its way back to me, you do not come back without that radio. Come back without it, and I will court martial you. Understood?'

'Perfectly, sir,' Callaghan said, before ducking out the tent into the glare of the autumn morning sun.

The pair urgently tramped through the camp in search of Jenkins. They made their way through the prostrate bodies, either dozing or smoking or cleaning their weapons.

They found him leaning against a supply truck, eating breakfast from a can with a fork. Jenkins was tall and spindly, with a pale, gaunt face. Callaghan often thought he looked worried, even when he was enjoying himself, like a schoolboy who'd forgotten his homework and feared the consequences to come. But for all that, Callaghan had grown close to him during their evening card games, and he'd always stuck up for him when the rest of the group had mocked his pathetic wispy moustache and threatened to pin him down and shave it off.

'What the fuck was that all that about?' Callaghan said.

'He's told you, has he?' Jenkins replied, and he stopped eating.

'Sounds like a suicide mission to me.' Callaghan looked at Baxter when he said it, and then back at Jenkins. 'Why the hell did you put us forward?'

'I didn't. Douglas-Sykes and Shawcroft did that. You were top of Shawcroft's list to go until I got you bumped down. I had hoped the others would be back by now.'

'But Maynard and Hinchcliffe only went yesterday.'

'Yes, but the Matthews brothers left early on Tuesday morning and Freddy went with McFadyen on Wednesday. I got my orders to keep it quiet so I couldn't tell you.'

'You've got to be kidding me.'

'You're the fourth pair to go, but Shawcroft wanted you to go on Tuesday until I talked him out of it.'

'So that's why Freddy wasn't about for cards last night.'

Baxter cut in, 'And we've heard nothing from any of them?'

'Nothing.'

Callaghan stared at the floor with his hands on his hips, but when he glanced up to see Baxter's worried face, he put a hand on his shoulder.

'We'll be alright, Bax,' Callaghan said. 'We'll play it safe; any sign of trouble and we'll get out of there. We can shift quickly if we need to. You've got our packs, Jenkins?'

Jenkins tossed his tin on the ground and went to the back of the truck to collect two pre-prepared kit bags.

'You've got extra rations, a week's worth, and extra ammo and I've given you each five grenades. You get a Sten as well.'

'Do we?' Callaghan said. 'Bloody hell, it must be dangerous. Bax, you take it, but keep your rifle as well.'

When he gave Baxter the machine gun, Jenkins said quietly to Callaghan, 'Bill, listen. Fuck the radio. Forget about it. If there's any chance of getting hold of it, one of the other pairs will have it by now. Just don't get caught in that retreat. Head west to begin with, go west for at least five miles before you turn north, get around the back of that column before you go looking for the Yanks.'

'Did you say that to all the others?'

'No, just you.'

Callaghan thought it over before saying, 'Durrant still owes me from cards the other night, and you can tell him I'm coming back for it.'

Jenkins snatched a handful of chocolate bars out of the truck and stuffed them into Baxter's backpack. 'Get going as soon as you can,' he said. 'Keep it secret and remember what I said.'

The two soldiers gathered up the rest of their things from the pits they'd slept in and, without saying goodbye to anyone, they walked out of camp to follow their compass north.

Callaghan led the way, using his rifle to push the uncut wheat to one side as they moved forward. It occurred to him, in the peaceful silence of an early Flanders morning, that this was the first time since they had landed in France together, that he and Baxter had been away from the group, away from the noise and the fear and the bickering.

When their battalion was out of sight, Callaghan stopped. 'What do you think about what Jenkins said, Bax? About heading west.'

'I don't know, Bill. What do you think?'

'It's tempting, that's for sure,' Callaghan said. 'I'd be lying if I said it wasn't. We head west now for four or five miles and there's no chance we'll see that retreat, but I don't know, it just doesn't feel right. Somebody's got to get that radio. Douglas-Sykes will just keep on sending pairs out until he gets it. I think we should keep going, head north, but I'd understand if you didn't want to.'

'Alright, Bill,' said Baxter. 'Let's keep going. Let's get that radio. I'd love to see the look on the captain's face when you give it to him.'

Callaghan laughed and they pressed ahead. After forty minutes, they emerged from the field of crops onto a small track where they found an abandoned wooden cart without its horse. Callaghan climbed up to stand on the cart's seat, where he surveyed the surroundings. He checked his compass to find the track ran broadly east–west. The topography was more or less flat in every direction and a fallow field of chopped-up soil lay ahead to the immediate north before green meadows stretched away to the horizon. The sun had now risen to take the early morning chill from the air, and it shimmered on a stream which, along with a string of trees, bound the western side of the soil field.

He remembered seeing the stream on the map and how it extended up until the road they were looking for. 'Alright, Bax,' he said. 'That way is north. Let's get over by those trees, so they give us some cover.'

They crossed the stream and followed it for more than three hours until they saw the road. A small bridge crossed the steam and the major road that Callaghan had envisaged turned out to be little more than a dirt track lined on either side by a straggly thicket.

When they reached the bridge they saw the wreckage, half a mile ahead as the land gently fell away into a trough. A non-armoured people-carrying truck with a soft-skin roof had turned over into a ditch and just behind it lay a tank, still upright but burnt out.

'They're not ours, are they?' Baxter asked.

'No, definitely not,' Callaghan replied. 'The tank looks like a Panzer, one of the older models, and it looks like it's been there for some time.'

Callaghan didn't like the idea of approaching directly down the road. 'Let's go around just in case,' he said. He took out his knife to cut back the hedge and force his way through into the meadow behind, and when Baxter followed, they made their way towards the vehicles.

25 yards out from the carnage, Callaghan slung his rifle

over his shoulder and drew his pistol. He signalled to Baxter, who readied the Sten.

When they reached the thicket, the stench of rotting corpses filled Callaghan's nostrils, and he peered through the shredded canvas canopy to see the pile of mangled bodies inside the truck. Callaghan climbed through the hedge and down into the ditch to take a closer look.

'They're all long dead,' he called out to Baxter. 'Seven of them, looks like an attack from the air. They didn't even get out the van. They must have been here for at least a couple of weeks, probably more. Too long to be part of that retreat. Let's take a look at the Panzer.'

Something grazed the road and kicked up a ball of dust as Baxter walked over to the tank.

Callaghan watched the cloud of dust disperse in the breeze before he grasped what it was. 'Baxter, get down,' he screamed.

Both men dived for cover, low in behind the tracks of the Panzer. Another bullet clattered the metal above them and Callaghan realised he'd misread the trajectory of the first shot. The shooter must be up in the trees, up on the higher ground to the east, and they were on the wrong side of the tank, exposed with only the hedgerow partially obscuring the sniper's line of sight if they stayed low enough.

'Bax,' he hissed frantically, 'get around the other side.'

Baxter lurched backwards as a bullet smashed into the tracks in front of him, and another shot crashed into the tank as he scampered around.

Callaghan had no choice but to dive past the point where the last slug had just struck. He held his breath as he lunged forward, knowing if the shooter held his line, he was dead. The shot came, too high, and Callaghan flinched as it ricocheted off the tank's armour.

Baxter had crouched down low and pressed his back up against the tank, and when Callaghan joined him, he did the same.

'We're trapped,' Baxter said. 'What do we do, Bill?'

Callaghan knew immediately they only had one way out. 'We cut our way through the hedge,' he said, pointing, 'just here where we're hidden by the tank. The hedge is thick enough and if we keep low, we'll be out of sight. There's a farm further up there on our side and we can take shelter there. We need to do it quickly, in case they're moving in on us. OK?'

'Alright,' Baxter agreed, 'let's do it.'

The soldiers leapt forward and hacked their way through the thicket, and when they had broken through, they scurried away on hands and knees behind the hedgerow.

The farm proved to be further away than Callaghan had expected, but by the time they reached it, he knew they had put enough distance between themselves and the sniper.

They got to their feet and walked into the farm. Judging from the crushed wooden fences and neglected timber-framed barns and outbuildings, Callaghan suspected tanks had rolled through the farm when the Germans had advanced at the outset of the war, and the place had been deserted ever since.

They passed a rusting metal hopper outside a stone building with a pitched roof, and Callaghan asked, 'Are you hungry, Bax?'

'I was hungry,' Baxter said, 'but I'm not now. My heart's still pounding after that. I could do with a drink, though.'

They walked around a barn and into the farm's central courtyard, where they saw a circle of soldiers lounging around a fire. A suspended wrought-iron cooking pot dangled from a frame and the smell of food now caught the air.

Callaghan heard a panicked voice shouting from inside the barn. He didn't understand the words, but he knew what they meant.

7

THATCHAM, ENGLAND, 1986

The following Friday night, Aunty Flo phoned to let us know she'd arrive at 11am on Saturday morning. At 6pm she still hadn't shown.

We subsequently found out, from the report published in the local newspaper the following week, the incident occurred at 3:17pm.

Her train pulled into Thatcham station at 10:25am and she'd declined Nan's offer for Larry to pick her up, by saying she'd prefer to make her own way rather than put Larry out.

11am came and went and we waited throughout the day without any news until 6:02pm, when a commotion at the back door set the dogs barking.

Nan got to the door first, opened it and said rather abruptly, 'Have you been in the pub all day?'

'Hello, Bet. Hello, Jamie.' Aunty Flo beamed. 'No, not all day. I've been down the bookies and at the police station for some of it.'

'This is James, or PC Burrows, I should say,' she went on, introducing the young, fresh-faced police officer standing next to her. He was carrying two suitcases and had a third wedged under his arm. 'He very kindly offered to drop me back.'

Aunty Flo waltzed in with PC Burrows traipsing behind with the cases.

'So, what's happened then?' Nan asked, but Aunty Flo wasn't listening.

She came over to me and whispered, 'How did the football finish? It was one–one with about ten to go when I last saw.'

'We lost two–one. They scored with five minutes to go, and they said on the TV it looked offside as well.'

'We lost? How the hell did we lose to that lot? They're bottom of the league, aren't they? That's it, Jamie, they've got to sack him now.'

PC Burrows cleared his throat. 'Where would you like me to put these?' he asked, lifting up the suitcases.

'Just over there, love,' Nan said, 'in the dining room.'

'And then you must join us for a cup of tea,' Aunty Flo announced.

PC Burrows put the cases down. 'No, I can't,' he said, glancing towards the door. 'I've got to get back to the station.'

'No, no, I insist,' Aunty Flo said. She grabbed his elbow and tugged him towards the dining room table. 'Jamie, be a dear and make us all some tea, will you?'

Aunt Flo sat PC Burrows down. He perched awkwardly on his chair, towering over the two tiny frail old ladies who'd positioned themselves on either side. He was tall with broad shoulders, and he must have weighed more than both of them put together.

From the kitchen I heard him ask, 'Are you two twins?'

'No,' Aunty Flo said. 'Sisters, but not twins. I'm actually 18 months older, although, to look at us, you'd think she was the older one, wouldn't you?'

'Thank you very much,' Nan said. 'You're full of compliments today. And I suppose you want one of these?' She held out an open pack of cigarettes. PC Burrows declined, but Aunty Flo took one.

'Right,' Nan said, lighting her cigarette, 'are you going to tell us what happened or what?'

'Well,' Aunty Flo said dismissively, 'there was a little disagreement in the bookies.'

'A mass brawl,' PC Burrows chimed in, anticipating the wording we would later read in the newspaper report, but when Aunty Flo cut him a look, he sank back in his chair.

'There was a misunderstanding,' Aunty Flo said. 'It was all a fuss about nothing really. I had a few quid on the Quarryman in the 2:15pm at Sandown Park and a few of the others in The King's Head had come in with me. It romped home by four lengths and my betting slip clearly said 9/2, but the idiot in the bookies insisted it was a 7 and not a 9 and when he paid out for 7/2, a couple of the guys from the pub were a little miffed. One thing led to another and the next thing I knew, James and his colleagues, who I must say did a splendid job, were in the thick of it trying to calm things down.'

'So why did you end up down the police station?' Nan asked.

'Just to help out with some paperwork.'

'Two men ended up in hospital,' PC Burrows said, 'so we took statements from all witnesses in case anyone decides to press charges.'

'But,' Aunty Flo said, 'they did pay out on 9/2 in the end, so everything worked out and justice was served.'

I arrived with the tea and joined them at the table.

Nan didn't say anything, and her expression gave nothing away, but I knew full well that Aunty Flo had form when it came to disputes with bookmakers. Under circumstances that sounded all too familiar, she had once been banned from all the betting shops on Hayling Island.

'They just don't like losing,' Aunty Flo had protested under questioning from Nan. 'They don't have a problem taking your money, but when you hit a winning streak and they've got to pay out, it all turns nasty. Anyway, they have apologised to me and accepted it was a misunderstanding and I have been reinstated. And do you want to know the best thing about it? My first bet when they'd let me back in was Diamond Tap in the 3:40pm at Haydock Park. It was losing all the way but nicked it by a nose at the line and, best of all, it was the 25/1 outsider. You should have seen the look on their faces.'

'You're not Gail's son by any chance, are you?' Nan asked PC Burrows.

'Yes, that's right.'

'I thought as much. I can see the resemblance. You look just like her. I know her from bingo, but she's obviously not been for a while. How's the treatment going?'

'It's going well, thank you,' PC Burrows said. 'The doctors are pleased with her and she's hoping to get back to bingo soon.'

'That's nice to hear. Hopefully I'll see her there.'

'Sorry, but can I ask your name?' PC Burrows asked.

'Of course, love. It's Mrs Callaghan, Betty Callaghan. She'll know who I am if you say you saw me.'

'Callaghan?' PC Burrows said, grabbing at his chin. 'There's something about the name that rings a bell.'

'Maybe your mum has mentioned me?' Nan said. 'We usually see each other and chat when we meet up at bingo.'

'No, it's not that.' He looked at me but directed his question at Nan, 'You have children, a son maybe, that I know from somewhere?'

'I did have a son, but he died a long time ago.'

'Oh, I'm very sorry.'

'Its fine, love. Don't worry.'

'I need the loo,' Aunty Flo said. She got to her feet and headed upstairs.

PC Burrows hesitated. The puzzled look on his face told me he had more questions, but he seemed afraid to ask them. After thinking it over, he finally asked, 'Perhaps it's your sister's son that I know?'

'No, love,' Nan said. 'You won't know her son either. They had a falling out and she's not seen him for years now. None of us have, for that matter. It's best not to mention it.'

'I'm sorry, I didn't mean to—'

'It's alright, love. Don't give it a second thought. Families can be complicated, even the closest ones. Now tell me about you and, what's your girlfriend's name, Eve is it? You're engaged, aren't you? Have you got a date in mind for the wedding?'

'Yes, next summer,' PC Burrows said.

The conversation went on, but I lost interest in it as

my thoughts drifted away towards Aunty Flo's son Conor and the reason why she's had fallen out with him. Nan had always refused to discuss it with me. Aunty Flo took her time, and when she did return, she didn't sit down until she'd determined what was being discussed.

'Are you OK, Aunty Flo?' I whispered while Nan spoke to PC Burrows. 'Is your tea alright?'

'Yes, dear,' she replied quietly. 'Shame about the football today though. We're at home next week, aren't we? I'll take you up if you want to go. Skinny Pete's out now and back on the turnstiles, so he'll slip us in for nothing. Do you fancy it?'

'Yes, please.'

'Good stuff. Oh and before I forget, you need to take the 24th off school. It's a Friday. I need you to come out with me for the day. I've agreed it with your nan.'

'What for?'

'A little adventure,' she said vaguely. She'd been looking down her nose at her tea without drinking any and now she pushed it away. 'Get me a port and lemon, will you, Jamie?'

When I returned with Aunty Flo's drink, PC Burrows had risen to his feet. 'Well, it's been nice talking to you all, but I really must get back to the station,' he said.

'It's been nice talking to you as well, love,' Nan said. 'Pass on my best to your mum when you see her.'

Nan saw him to the door but before he left, she asked, 'How are things at the station these days? It must be strange with Sergeant Meadows retiring. When does he leave?'

'Just before Christmas,' PC Burrows replied. 'He's been on the force for 39 years.'

'Is it really that long? Going back a while now, long

before your time, a lot of people around here considered him a hero. I thought he might have stuck around to make it 40 years of service. Unless it's not his choice he's leaving of course?'

'Oh, I don't know about that,' PC Burrows said. 'I don't listen to any of that talk.'

'Very wise, love,' Nan said, 'very wise. You take good care now.'

8

I could never understand why Nan set the clock in the kitchen ten minutes fast. Every other clock and watch in the house would be wound to the correct time, but she insisted the kitchen clock had to be different.

'But it gives you an extra ten minutes to make sure you're never late,' she would say with a look of disbelief, finding it impossible to understand why I didn't agree. 'You hate being late, Jamie. Remember how upset you always get.'

'I know,' I'd say, 'but why can't we just set it to the right time and leave ten minutes early?'

'But the kitchen clock gives us an extra ten minutes. I really don't see what all the fuss is about.'

'But surely—'

'We're not changing it,' she'd snap, and I'd give up until the next time the clocks changed.

When Aunty Flo moved in, I took the opportunity to recruit an ally. On the Sunday morning after she'd arrived, I was due at Larry's to help in the garden at 9am. I set my alarm to 8am and when I went down for breakfast, I found her sat reading at the dining room table with a cup of tea and smoke from her cigarette curling up to the ceiling. Given the amount of port she'd drunk the night before, I didn't expect to see her up so early, but she greeted me with a cheerful, 'Morning, Jamie.'

I explained the clock situation.

'It doesn't make any sense, does it? You agree with me, don't you, Aunty Flo?'

'No, I do not,' Aunty Flo shot back without lifting her eyes from the *Racing Post*. 'The kitchen clock gives you an extra ten minutes. I really don't see what all the fuss is about, dear.'

I got to Larry's five minutes early, or five minutes late, going by our kitchen clock.

I knocked twice on the front door, but it didn't open. Instead of answering the door, Larry appeared at the gate to the side of his house.

His navy-blue paint-splattered overalls and thick grey hair, combed back from his forehead, reminded me of Grandad.

'Come on through, Jamie,' he said, 'we've already started. Not too wet and windy for you, is it?'

As I followed him through the gate and down the damp passage along the side of his house, I puzzled over the "we've already started" phrase he'd used.

I'd assumed it would be just the two of us, and the thought of working with somebody I didn't know brought an uneasy feeling. I hoped it had been a slip of the tongue.

At the back of the house, the passage opened out into a long garden of patchy grass, bound on all sides by a rickety timber fence.

Numerous wooden slats were broken or missing from the fence and a dense, overgrown bramble sprawled across the rear boundary, a small part of which had already been cut down and lay in a heap on the lawn.

To my right, the door of a timber shed had been left open and inside and I saw a pile of black sacks propped up against a petrol lawnmower. I guessed the bramble had to be cleared and the bags would be used to dispose of it. It looked like a mammoth task for the two of us.

'Hello, Jamie,' came a gentle voice from behind me.

Suddenly, I turned around and Freya was standing there, framed in the doorway to Larry's kitchen. Her hair had been tied up into two pig tails and her fringe seemed to be longer than usual, half covering her eyes.

She wore yellow dungarees over a thick, knitted, navy-blue jumper with the sleeves folded back and dirty grey gloves, clearly too big for her hands, dangling from the ends of her arms.

'Hello, Jamie,' she said again.

'Hello,' I uttered back.

Larry asked me, 'Are you alright?'

I nodded and he handed me a pair of gloves, every bit as dirty and oversized as those Freya had on.

I pulled on the gloves to feel their cold, abrasive inner lining against my skin and as I did so, a gale threw the shed door back as far as its hinges could stretch. It was only then, when the noise of the door swinging in the wind diverted my attention, did it occur to me I'd been staring at Freya the whole time.

'Alright, you two,' Larry said, as he strolled to the rear of the garden, 'let's get to work.'

Freya came bounding past and, out of the corner of my eye, I caught a glimpse of her smiling at me as she skipped ahead.

At the bottom of the garden, Larry gave us instructions and then he climbed up a timber stepladder where, from halfway up, he used a pair of long-handled loppers to cut back the bushes before chucking the offcut branches into a heap.

Freya and I, both armed with rusty secateurs, worked through the pile, chopping the bramble down into smaller pieces before stuffing it into the black sacks.

Each time we managed to clear the pile, we'd share a smile and carry the collection of sacks we'd packaged up around the house to the front garden, where Larry told us he'd arranged for Pete Mulligan to pick everything up in his van on Monday morning.

We worked in silence, and I desperately wanted to say something funny or clever, but when nothing came to me, I thought it best to keep quiet.

During one trip along the side passage, Freya's sack split where a branch had sliced through the black plastic. I said, 'Freya, stop, wait here,' and I raced back to get another bag. Together, we pulled the second sack up around the first and I helped her wrestle it out into the front garden.

'Thanks, Jamie,' she said, as we dumped the bag next to the others. She made a movement, and, for a moment, I thought she wanted to kiss my cheek to thank me, but she simply straightened and left me hovering, hunched over.

I stood upright and said, 'That's no problem,' trying to hide my embarrassment.

She slipped away and I followed after her down the

passage, hoping she hadn't noticed. At the time, I deluded myself that she didn't notice, but reflecting on it now, years later, I am left in no doubt I made a complete fool of myself.

We continued to work through the morning and with almost two thirds of the fence cleared of bramble, Larry said, 'Alright, I think it's time for lunch.'

I checked my watch. One o'clock sharp.

Larry's kitchen provided shelter from the wind, but it was no warmer inside than in the garden. He sat us on high stools in the corner and peeled the tin foil off a plate of jam sandwiches he must have made earlier that morning.

'I hope you like jam,' he said. 'Your nan made it for me, Jamie.'

I hadn't realised how hungry I was until we began to eat, and as we ate the sandwiches, my eyes scanned around Larry's house. In the dim light from the overcast skies outside, I determined the structural layout was identical to our house, but the similarities went no further.

Except for the counter we sat at, the two cupboards under the sink, a fridge and a white ceramic cooker with black scorch marks and a missing dial, the kitchen felt empty and gave the impression of being twice the size of ours.

From my position, I could see through the arch to the dining room, and through the door at the end of the room into the lounge, and both appeared to be as equally sparse as the kitchen.

An assortment of fishing equipment occupied one wall of the empty dining room and in the lounge, I could make out no more than a threadbare two-seater sofa positioned in front of a wooden-cased TV.

In both rooms, the grey-and-brown patterned carpet

didn't fully extend out to the perimeter walls, instead dissolving into frayed edges with tufts of underlay poking through.

Larry placed two yellow plastic beakers in front of us and filled them with orange squash from a jug he'd taken out of the fridge. I drained the beaker in one and Larry topped it up.

'Well done, you two,' he said, 'good work this morning.'

I couldn't help but notice the house didn't have any plants, pictures or ornaments, but my attention kept reverting to a small metallic clock with a black face positioned on top of the television.

A lorry passed noisily by in the street outside and the change of light reflected off its glazed fascia.

'Do you like it?' Larry asked me as I stared past him. 'The clock. Do you like it?'

'Yes,' I said.

Moving more quickly than he usually did, he limped over to the TV and brought it back. He handed it to me and said, 'It's a very special clock.'

The cylindrical clock itself measured no more than 12 or 13 centimetres across and it had been mounted on a dark-brown varnished plaque with a slight incline.

In addition to the conventional numbers and hands of a clock, the clock face was littered with additional numbers, dials and scales.

'Is it for experiments?' Freya asked.

'No,' said Larry, 'but it's not your normal clock.'

Freya pointed to the protruding button positioned on the top above the number twelve. 'Is that a stopwatch?'

'Yes, that's right,' Larry said.

I passed it to Freya so she could take a closer look. 'Where's it from?' I asked.

'It was given to me a long time ago,' Larry said.

Freya pressed the stopwatch button and one of the dials reset to zero before starting to rotate again.

I sensed Larry had more to say, but for some reason he hesitated. As Freya examined the clock, I glanced up into Larry's face.

He said quietly and carefully, 'Your grandad gave it to me, Jamie. He knew I'd like it, so he gave it to me as a present.'

I felt Freya's eyes on me as I processed Larry's words. She gave the clock back to him and he examined it before placing it on the fridge.

'It was all a long time ago,' he said, and I thought I saw tears welling in his eyes.

'Right then,' he said, standing up straight and clapping his hands against his sides as if to draw a line under the conversation.

He picked up a sandwich, his first, and before taking a bite, he said, 'Finish your drinks, you two, and let's get back out there.'

We returned to the garden and worked until ten to four, when the sky darkened and heavy rain began to fall. We'd watched black clouds drift in from the east and we tried to work faster to get finished before they reached us.

'Inside, you two,' Larry shouted against the driving rain.

'But, Larry,' Freya protested, 'we're nearly finished.'

'Let us carry on, Larry,' I hollered over the noise of the rain crashing down on the shed roof. 'We can do it; we can get it finished.'

'No, no, come on, you two, inside,' Larry shouted back.

He took the secateurs from our hands and wrapped his arms around our shoulders to guide us back inside.

We fell in through the kitchen door and I closed it to shut out the storm.

'Look at you both,' Larry said, 'you're absolutely soaked.'

'But it was fun,' Freya said, shaking the rain from her hair. 'We nearly got there, we could have finished.'

'I can't thank you enough,' Larry said. 'You've both been such a big help.'

He told us he'd finish up the last bit in the morning before Pete Mulligan came by, and then he handed over two envelopes with our names on, scribbled in blue ink.

'These are for you,' he said. 'You've both earned every penny. Hold back a few minutes until the weather clears and then you can head on home.'

We thanked Larry. Freya climbed up onto a stool and leant on the windowsill to watch the rain beat down outside and I did the same.

The downpour fell steadily, but the constant rhythm was interrupted by an occasional change of wind which brought a splatter on the window from the broken gutter above.

I said to Freya, 'Did you see that?' and I pointed to a flash of lightning over the rooftops.

She nodded and smiled, and the thunder grumbled all around us.

The clouds shifted from left to right. In time, brighter skies lifted the gloom and when I looked to the west I briefly glimpsed the faint outline of the sinking sun through the pale-grey haze.

I had lost all track of time when Larry said, 'Alright, you

two, it's a bit better out there now; best make a dash for it while you can.'

We said our goodbyes, but when Freya opened the door, I felt Larry's hand on my shoulder.

'It's time for you to have this, Jamie.' He pressed the clock into my hand. 'Please don't argue,' he said. 'I won't be around forever and it's time to pass it on.'

'Are you sure?'

'Yes, please take it. And thank you both for everything.'

I stuffed my envelope in a pocket, and I held the base of the clock's plaque with both hands.

Walking behind Freya along the soggy passage, it occurred to me I would soon be alone with her and keen to avoid an uncomfortable silence, I urgently searched for something to say.

I still had nothing when I drew alongside her in the street but, to my relief, she asked me, 'Who's that lady at your house? Is she your nan's sister? She must be. They look so similar.'

'How did you know she was with us?' I asked. 'She only arrived yesterday.'

'She arrived in a police car. Everyone in the street saw her arrive.'

'That's true,' I conceded.

'She looks like fun,' Freya went on. 'I think she was telling the police officer a joke; he was laughing, anyway. And she was quite noisy.'

'Yes, she can be quite loud.'

Freya stopped walking so I did the same and we stood facing each other in the rain.

Further up Paynesdown Road, I could see my house, but

we'd pulled up just before hers had come into view and I realised she'd be in a great deal of trouble if her dad saw us together.

'I'm sorry your grandad died,' she said unexpectedly.

'And I'm sorry your mum died.'

Freya pushed her wet fringe to one side. 'Me too,' she said. 'I want to go and live with my aunt and uncle in Ipswich, but I'm not allowed.'

Not for the first time, I thought over what it must be like for her to live alone with her father, and I didn't know what to say.

A car came around the bend with its headlights in our eyes.

I tugged at Freya's arm to pull her back from the curb, so the car didn't splash us as it sped by.

'Did your mum and dad die as well?' she asked, when the car had driven past.

'Yes, a long time ago,' I said.

'I'm sorry,' she said, and I could tell she had more questions, but decided not to ask them.

Neither of us spoke, but it wasn't awkward.

Freya turned towards her house. 'I guess we've got to go home now.'

'Yes, I guess,' I replied, grateful that Nan, Aunty Flo, and the dogs were waiting for me.

'I want you to have this,' I said, and I pushed the clock into her hand before backing away a few paces so she couldn't give it back.

She called out to object, but I couldn't hear what she said above the noisy exhaust of an old van passing by.

I jogged backwards, and through a smile I shouted,

'I want you to have it. It's yours. I'll see you tomorrow at school.'

I crossed the road and glanced over my shoulder. She hadn't moved and in the headlights of a car she raised a hand to wave goodbye.

Back at home, I peeled off my soaking coat and jumper and bounded into the lounge to find Nan and Aunty Flo watching an old black-and-white film. Two navy officers were arguing on the deck of a battleship.

'Guess what?' I said. 'Freya was at Larry's too.'

'Jamie, shhhh,' Aunty Flo hissed back, straining to hear the TV, 'this is a good bit.'

'Nan,' I whispered, 'we got loads done. And Larry gave us some money.'

'That's nice, love.'

'And guess what? Freya was there too.'

'Oh really,' she said with her knitting needles clicking frantically. 'That was a nice surprise then.'

Stan had leapt down from the settee to greet me when I came in. For a few moments he sniffed around my socks and the bottoms of my jeans, all of which were wet through, and then, unimpressed, he jumped up again.

'Jamie?' Aunty Flo looked over her glasses at me. 'Did you put the kettle on when you came in?'

Nan said, 'This finishes in a minute, love. Make us a quick cup of tea and at five o'clock that programme you wanted to watch is on.'

The kitchen clock had already struck five. I filled the kettle and emptied out the teapot and with the kitchen clock running fast, I knew I had an extra ten minutes before my programme started.

9

Much to my disappointment, I didn't see Freya at school the next day.

Earlier that morning, I had woken from a dream of blustering winds and wet sand between my toes, and she immediately entered my thoughts.

Whilst cleaning my teeth after breakfast, I rehearsed what I planned to say to her about our day together with Larry and as I walked to school, I repeated the exercise in my mind.

We didn't cross paths throughout the morning, but that was not unusual for a Monday, and at lunchtime I left my friends to their game of football on the tennis courts and went to search for her.

I mistakenly thought I saw the back of Freya's head through a crowd as it filed out of the science block, but as I drew closer, I realised it was a girl in the year above with the same colour hair.

One of her friends said brusquely, 'What do you want?' but the disgruntled look on my face must have sent the girl away wondering what she'd done to offend me.

At the end of the day, with my confidence all but extinguished, I loitered at the school gates, hoping for one final chance to intercept Freya on her way home.

I waited until 3:50pm and then traipsed home alone.

As it turned out, Freya didn't attend school all that week and I began to worry why.

After I'd returned home on Friday, Aunty Flo sank into her armchair as I sat brooding in front of the TV.

'So, what's wrong with you then?' she asked.

'Nothing.'

'Don't give me all that. What is it?'

'It's nothing, there's nothing wrong.'

'Come on, you can trust me. Tell me what's wrong and we'll sort it out.'

Nan came in from the kitchen wearing her bright-yellow marigolds. 'What's going on?'

Aunty Flo tilted her head in my direction. 'I'm trying to cheer this one up.'

'Everything's fine,' I said, a little too defensively. 'I don't need cheering up.'

'Alright, love,' Nan said. She sat down next to me on the sofa, picked up her packet of cigarettes from the table, and took one out. 'We believe you. Just let us know if you do ever need anything. We might be old, but I'm sure we can still give you some sensible advice.'

She snapped out a flame from her lighter and lit her cigarette. 'Well, I can anyway.'

Aunty Flo shot me a sceptical look but, thankfully, she changed tack. 'Talking of sensible advice, Jamie. Your nan has decided to take some from me. We've got some news for you. Chuck us a fag, Bet.'

'Wait a minute.' Nan coughed. 'I've not agreed to that yet.'

She threw a cigarette at Aunty Flo, who tried to catch it in her mouth, but it bounced from her top lip and fell into her lap.

'Alright, alright,' Aunty Flo said. 'We're still just thinking about it, but we might be getting a lodger.'

I looked at them both in turn. 'What? What do you mean?'

'We might be getting a lodger,' my aunt said again.

'A lodger? That would live here with us. All the time?'

'It's not definite,' Nan said, 'but they'd pay rent, and the money would come in useful.'

Aunty Flo lit her cigarette. 'We'd be mad not to,' she said, exhaling smoke. 'It makes perfect sense. The extra money we'd get, on top of our pensions and my money from the horses, would mean your nan wouldn't have to work and we'd have a bit left over to go to the bingo every night if we wanted to. And we might even have enough for a little holiday.'

'But where will they sleep?' I asked.

'My room,' said Aunty Flo. 'And I'll be moving in with your nan.'

'That's the problem,' Nan said. 'I've spent far too much of my life sharing a bedroom with her, I can tell you.'

'Don't start on about that again, that problem has been solved, and you know it,' Aunty Flo said. She then turned to me. 'I know a guy in The Cricket's who's a chippy, he's going to build us a partition with a door to divide up the room. I gave him a nice little tip on the gee-gees last week, so he said he'd do it for nothing.' She paused for a drag and then flicked the ash into the ashtray balanced on the arm of her chair. 'What do you think, then?'

I thought it over and gave the answer I felt I should. 'I think it's a good idea, especially if you can give up work, Nan.'

'Thanks, love. It's nice of you to say that.'

'There we go then,' Aunty Flo said. 'All agreed. You know what, I think I might have a little drink tonight.'

'You have a little drink every night,' Nan said, but Aunty Flo ignored her.

'Yes, I think I'll have a little drink tonight. Oh, and in case I forget to mention it, Neil's coming over on Monday for dinner, so we can all get to know each other.'

'Is that right?' Nan said.

'And Larry's coming as well, Jamie, so you can set the table for five.'

Later that night, Nan and I tried to find out a bit more about our new lodger.

'There's nothing to say,' Aunty Flo said irritably during the TV adverts. 'He's basically a balding 24-year-old bloke who needs somewhere to live. What else do you need to know?'

Nan led the line of questioning. 'Where did you meet him?'

'The White Hart.'

'Where's he from?'

'Bath.'

'What's he doing here?'

'Working. He's an electrician. His company moved him here.'

'So, where's he living at the moment?'

'In one of the rooms above The White Hart.'

'And he wants somewhere more permanent?'

'Yep.'

Aunty Flo's mood grew increasingly tetchy with every question. In between each one, she'd take a long, nonchalant pull on her cigarette before tipping her head back to blow smoke rings up to the ceiling.

I had questions to get in before she blew up completely. 'Does he like football? And what team does he support?'

'No, he doesn't like football, he likes rugby.'

'Rugby?'

'Yes, rugby. And steam engines and brewing his own beer. That's it, alright. Is there anything else you'd like to know?'

Nan said, 'Nope, that will be all. It'll be interesting to meet him.'

Aunty Flo uttered something under her breath before saying, 'Right, I need a refill.'

While I tried to work out if a steam engine was an old-fashioned train or a tractor with a big rolling wheel at the front, she testily stubbed out her cigarette, drained the Guinness from her glass and headed to the kitchen.

I whispered to Nan, 'What's wrong with her?'

'She's nervous, love. She gets like this. It's now dawned on her that Neil is actually moving in and she's worried we won't like him.'

'But why is she so worried? She doesn't normally worry about stuff.'

'She must be really fond of him. She's always been the same, ever since she was a little girl. She's always had a thing for the runt of every litter.'

The phrase 'runt of every litter' left me the moment Nan had said it but it quickly returned the following Monday evening, when Aunty Flo guided Neil in the back door and introduced us.

'Here he is,' Aunty Flo announced loudly.

She thrust Neil out in front of her and his podgy cheeks flushed as he stood helplessly in the middle of the kitchen.

His nervous fingers fidgeted at the cuffs of an oversized duffel coat that must have been two sizes too big for him and the toggles at the front had been buttoned to the wrong holes, so one half of the coat hung lower than the other.

Nan, crouched down at the oven, looked up and greeted him with a smile. 'Hello, love. Nice to meet you.'

'Hello, Mrs Callaghan,' Neil replied in a broad West Country accent.

'Call me Betty, love.'

'And this is my nephew,' Aunty Flo said, 'the one I've been telling you about.'

'Hello, Danny.'

'Jamie,' Aunty Flo quickly corrected him.

Nan apologised on behalf of Larry, who couldn't make it as he'd gone to visit a friend in hospital, and she then told Neil we were having stew and dumplings. As she dished up, she listed the other meals she'd be cooking for him through the week, and he confirmed he liked everything she had planned.

From the corner of the kitchen, I watched Aunty Flo with fascination as the conversation unfolded. Her lips twitched when it was Neil's turn to speak, as though she wanted to reply for him, and she gave a subtle, satisfied nod of the head each time he successfully answered a question.

She sat him down next to her at the dining room table and when we were ready, she impatiently said, 'Come on, eat,' like the frustrated owner of a poodle, urging it to perform a new trick in front of friends.

'So, you've just moved here from Bath then, Neil?' Nan asked.

He finished his mouthful before replying. 'Yes, I was living at home there with my mother.'

Under interrogation over the weekend, Aunty Flo had already told us his dad had walked out on them years ago when Neil was a child.

'And I understand your company moved your job up this way?'

'Yes, that's right,' Neil said. 'I had to move out from home and most of our work is in London and around here anyway, so they said they'd pay some expenses if I moved here.'

'That was good of them,' Nan said. 'How come you had to move out?'

'My mother's new boyfriend lives there now, so there isn't room for me anymore.'

Nan looked embarrassed. 'I'm sorry to hear that, love.'

'Oh, that's all in the past.' Aunty Flo gave a dismissive wave of her fork. 'He's got us now. He doesn't need anyone else, and he certainly doesn't need her. Jamie, permission to swear?'

Aunty Flo had set up some rules with me about swearing on the train as we travelled to football one day. 'Don't give me that look you normally do,' she had said. 'It's perfectly acceptable to swear at football, Jamie. Passions run high and sometimes there's just no other way to tell the ref what you think of him.'

She used the ref as an example, but it was the opposition's players, and in particular their fans in the terrace away to our left, who usually took the brunt of her abuse. In the terms of our agreement, however, it was all perfectly acceptable. Anyone in that stadium was fair game.

'But no swearing when we're not at football,' she had warned me, 'unless it's absolutely necessary and even then, we must ask each other for permission first. Deal?'

Across the dinner table, I consented to Aunty Flo's request, 'Permission to swear granted.'

'Well, I'm sorry but there's no getting away from it,' she said. 'Neil's mum is a fucking bitch, there it is, I've said it.'

Neil carried on eating, seemingly unsurprised or undisturbed by my aunt's outburst.

'I wish you'd watch your language, Florence,' Nan said calmly, pouring some gravy on her plate. 'You're in Berkshire now. We're not still back in London, you know.' She placed the gravy boat back in the middle of the table. 'Neil, I don't know anything about your family, love, but we'd be delighted if you'd stay here with us. You're welcome to stay as long as you like.'

Neil cleared his throat and readied himself to speak. 'Mrs Callaghan—'

'Call me Betty.'

'Betty.'

'Yes, love?'

We waited in anticipation.

'Betty, is it possible to use up a bit of the shed for my home-brewing equipment?'

'I don't see why not,' Nan said. 'There's a load of Bill's old rubbish in there we can get rid of to make some room.

If you don't mind helping us get rid of it, perhaps we could use your van?'

'That would be fine,' Neil replied. 'Thank you.'

'It is any good?' Nan asked. 'Your home brew?'

'It's like drinking bath water,' Aunty Flo said as she reached for the gravy. 'Remember when three or four of us kids had to share the same hot water, and it was your turn to be the last one in?'

Unmoved by the criticism, Neil said, 'It's coming on nicely, thank you, Betty, but I am trying out some new improvements.'

'Well, I look forward to trying some,' Nan said. 'I'm sure it's very good.'

After a pudding of homemade rhubarb crumble and custard, Aunty Flo showed Neil upstairs so he could see his new room, and then she took him outside to the shed. Nan and I washed up and settled in front of the TV with the dogs.

'Nan,' I asked, 'is Neil anything like Aunty Flo's son, Conor?'

'No, love,' she said, 'they couldn't be more different.'

'Will she ever see Conor again?'

'No.' Nan shook her head as she knitted. 'There's no chance of that. Not now.'

'Why? What did he do?'

'It was a long time ago, Jamie. It's all forgotten now.'

'Did my dad like him?'

'What?'

'My dad, did he like Conor? If they were cousins, they must have grown up together when you and Aunty Flo lived in London?'

'When they were babies, maybe, but when they were older, they didn't spend much time together. They didn't have anything in common really.'

She held up her knitting to examine it more closely. She was working on a brown patterned cardigan for her brother Tom, and I got the impression it had gone wrong.

Returning to the TV, she screwed her face up and said, 'Oh, I don't like this. I'm sure that bloke's a wrong-un. Turn it over, love. Let's see what's on the other side.'

10

The 8:12am train arrived overcrowded with people going to work.

Aunty Flo jostled her way through the carriage and told an unsuspecting young man in a business suit, rather rudely, to move across the aisle.

When he did so, she nestled into his seat and patted the empty one next to her. 'That's better. Now we can sit together,' she said, before taking out the *Racing Post* and disappearing behind it until we reached Reading station.

At Reading we had to change for the train to Oxford.

'Why are we going to Oxford?' I had asked the night before, having completely forgotten she'd arranged for me to have the 24th off school to accompany her.

'I'm glad you asked me that,' she said before she sat me down on the sofa, lit a cigarette, and proceeded to tell me.

After she'd explained everything, I waited, half expecting her to say she'd been joking. I paused, but rather than laugh off her wild and outlandish tale, she turned her nose up at the television and said, 'Turn this bloody rubbish over will you.'

When the train jerked into Reading, Aunty Flo resurfaced and said, 'Boston Joe in the 2:15pm at Redcar and then we'll go for Kite Runner in the 2:40pm. We'll nip in the bookies en route and pick up our winnings on the way back.'

She jammed the paper into the bin in the vestibule, and we alighted to let the train continue on its way to London. We found a newsagent at the side of the old Victorian ticket station where she bought a packet of cigarettes and we agreed on lemon bonbons from the colourful selection of sweets, all stored in glass jars and displayed on shelves along the rear wall.

The kiosk manager, who had oily grey hair and a rolled-up cigarette stuck to his bottom lip, measured out the bonbons in his scales, tipped them into a white paper bag, and sealed the bag by holding two corners and spinning the sweets over the top twice.

After Aunty Flo had paid him, an underpass full of graffiti and disinfectant led us to Platform 8 where the 9:06am for Banbury arrived on time with a sweet burning smell from the brakes, not unlike scorched rubber, wafting up from the tracks as the train ground to a halt.

The train was almost empty and arranged like the old-fashioned ones you see in black-and-white films, with a corridor down one side and separate compartments, and we managed to find an empty compartment for ourselves.

Aunty Flo sat opposite me at the window. 'Bonbon?' she asked, holding out the open bag.

We took in the rooftops and chimneys and TV ariels as they rolled past and I eventually asked her, 'So whose funeral are we going to? Someone from the convent?'

'No, he didn't have anything to do with the convent, but he owned the house next door where a few of us girls were allowed to work. I loved it there, and I went back after the war and worked for him for years.'

'Did Nan work there too?'

'No, she was unlucky. She got stuck in the laundry at the convent. We had it easy compared to her. We just messed around most of the time, and then did a bit of cleaning and serving food and drinks and that kind of thing. Your nan has never let me forget it.'

'Nan didn't like it at the convent, did she?'

'No,' Aunty Flo said, as she dipped in the bag for another sweet, 'none of us did.'

'Then why did your mum and dad send you there?'

'They had no choice, dear. It was the war. London was getting bombed every night and all the kids got sent out to the country. It was just the way it was. And we had nowhere to live, two days before we got moved out, our street got bombed. Has your nan ever told you about that?'

'No. What happened?'

'We'd all slept down in the underground and when we came out the next day, the houses either side of ours were gone.'

'Gone?'

'Completely destroyed. Bombs had flattened them and there were just these piles of rubble left. Our house in the middle was fine, well, we thought it was fine. When all us kids went in and ran up the stairs, the whole house shook from side to side and this police constable came in and shouted at us. He said we had to get out in case it collapsed. We never saw that house again. They sent us to a shelter in

Kings Cross the next night and then me and your nan were packed off to Oxford. The whole street has been turned into flats now.'

'Your other brothers and sisters didn't go with you?'

'No, we were all split up. By then our older brothers and sisters had already been sent away to the army or to work in a factory, so we didn't see them anyway, and nobody could take in all the rest of us, so we all went to different places. Sid got sent to a farm in Kent and Sheila went to a family in the West Country, but me and your nan ended up at the convent.'

'You must have all been sad, getting separated like that.'

'I suppose so. I don't really remember, to tell you the truth. We just got on with it.'

The train flashed through a station without stopping and the ticket inspector, an elderly lady with glasses, a warm smile and brown hair tied up under her cap, came into our carriage to ask for our tickets. 'Another 25 minutes for Oxford,' she said politely before accepting a bonbon, pulling her sleeve down and moving onto the next car.

'What was it like at the convent?' I asked. 'Was it bad?'

'The convent was fine, beautiful actually, and the other girls were nice enough, but it was the nuns, they were the problem. They were all evil bitches. You'd think they'd be kind and treat people properly, wouldn't you, working for God and all that.'

'But what did they do?' I pressed her. In the last few minutes, Aunty Flo had already let on much more than Nan ever had, and with her trapped in this carriage with me for the next 25 minutes, I decided this could well be my one and only chance to find out what had really happened in the convent.

'They were just cruel,' she said. 'They'd do horrible things; horrible things for no reason and that's why we hated them. It was just all so unnecessary.'

'But what? What exactly?' I asked.

Aunty Flo considered the question for a long time and at one point, I had almost given up on an answer. When she did finally speak, she spoke with a hatred and a bitterness I'd never seen in her before.

'Gertrude Bannister,' she said. 'After all the things they did to us. All the beatings and the humiliation, the physical and mental abuse. That's the one thing I'll never forgive them for. What they did to poor Gertrude. Sister Radcliffe and Sister Hughes, they were the worst. They were the ringleaders, but the rest of them weren't much better.'

'What did they do?'

'They picked on her. I mean, they all did, not just Radcliffe and Hughes, but all the nuns, every single one of them. The rest of us talked about it. We wondered whether they had all got together for a meeting to discuss it, to agree on who they would torment. And they ended up choosing her, poor Gertrude. The funny thing was, some of the girls started bullying Gertrude at the beginning of her first term. She was small, and plain, and had mousy-brown hair with thick bottle-top glasses, so they picked on her. But that all stopped overnight when the nuns started harassing her.'

'What happened?'

'It was so strange. We couldn't work it out at first. If any of the girls did anything wrong, even the slightest little thing, they wouldn't punish the girl, they would punish

Gertrude instead. Why would they do that? Why single her out? What's the point?'

'But what did the nuns do to her?'

'They made her stand alone outside all by herself. There was this big courtyard in the middle of the buildings with grass and fountains. Our dorms up on the top floor overlooked it so we could all see her. She had to stand exactly in the middle for hours on end while the rest of us were either working or had some free time. Even if it was freezing cold or tipping it down with rain, she had to stand still in the middle of the lawn. The poor thing. We gave her what we could: extra petticoats, and jumpers, and hot-water bottles to keep her warm, but it didn't help much. After a couple of months, she looked ill. I don't think she was eating or sleeping properly. Some of the girls went to the nuns and said they were worried about her.'

'Did they stop?' I blurted out foolishly.

'No, they carried on. They carried on exactly as before and, in the end, they went too far. Clara found her early one morning in the bathroom in a pool of blood. Gertrude had broken a mirror and slashed at her wrist. Radcliffe called an ambulance, and I remember being surprised that she'd actually done that. It was the first time she'd ever done the right thing by one of the girls, and when the ambulance came, they took her away.'

'Did she die?'

'Don't know. They wouldn't tell us. All the girls were desperate to find out, but we weren't allowed to talk about it. Even to this day, we still don't know whether she lived or died. After the war, when we left the convent, a few of us tried again to find out what had happened. But there were no records, nothing. She had simply vanished. I guess sometimes in life things end up like that, where there is no neat and tidy ending we can accept and move on.'

'I think she lived,' I said with a swell of optimism. 'I think she lived, and she's had a happy life. She got married to a nice man and they have children, and they live in a cottage in the country with chickens in her garden that lay eggs.'

'I hope so, Jamie,' Aunty Flo said. 'It's a nice thought, isn't it?'

'Were the nuns nicer after that?'

'Oh no, the nuns didn't change. They were as bad as ever and they simply moved on to a different girl. This time it was Sally Woodford. But we had changed, us girls were different after that. That was when the fight back began. Bonbon?'

Aunty Flo sat back in her chair to enjoy her sweet. When the ticket inspector hurried by, Aunty Flo held out the open bag. With a wide grin, the friendly old lady doubled back and came into our carriage to take a sweet. 'I don't mind if I do,' the inspector said. 'They're rather good, aren't they?'

'How long to Oxford now?' I asked.

'About another 15 minutes,' she said, before leaving.

'Come on, Aunty Flo,' I said, 'tell me about the fight back.'

'It had been coming for a while. Me and your nan had talked about it already, but when we lost Gertrude, that was it. We knew we had to do something. I think we were guilty really, guilty we hadn't done more for her, so we set up a committee. We'd read in the newspapers about the French resistance. They were fighting back against the Nazis in France at the time, and we thought we could do the same. Sister Holmes always went to bed late. She'd do a final patrol of the dorms around one in the morning, so after that, we got the committee together. We lit some candles we'd smuggled out of the store cupboard and sneaked out of our dorms and crept up into the loft space. There were only seven of us at first: Cathy, Annie, Marie, the two Janes and me and your nan. We sat in a circle around our candles and your nan said a few words for Gertrude. I can't remember much of what she said. But there is one line that has always stayed with me. "God will know his angels from the sorrow in their hearts," which some French bloke had written in one of the books she'd read.'

'Nan read books?'

'Oh yeah, loads of them. She was always in the library when she had some free time.'

'But she's not religious? She told me she hates all that stuff because of the nuns.'

'I know, dear, but I think she just wanted to say something nice about Gertrude. Anyway, after we'd paid our respects, we got on with things and we elected the leader and came up with a name. We called ourselves "The Resistance". Silly really. But we thought it gave us an identity and we could say to the other girls, "join The Resistance," and it sounded as if we would actually go and do something to get back at the nuns.'

I asked eagerly, 'What did you do?'

'That was the thing.' Aunty Flo shrugged and opened out her hands. 'We didn't have a clue. At the beginning, it was all a bit tame. The first thing we did was put itching powder in the nun's beds. We all wanted to do more, but we couldn't think of anything. There were these red berries that grew on bushes in the garden with a powdery substance inside, and it would drive you mad if you got it on your skin. Marie worked in housekeeping, so when she made the nun's beds, we got her to sprinkle some of this powder under their covers. We thought it was funny to begin with, but the trouble was, we never knew whether it worked or not. So, we moved on to the next thing and that was my idea. Hughes had given me the cane for something. I can't even remember what it was, but I wanted to get her back. So, I got Clara to sneak two fish fillets out of the kitchen and I then gave them to Marie to hide in Hughes' room. She hid one of the fish at the back of her wardrobe. When it started to stink, we knew she would find it. But this is the clever bit. She hid the second one under the floorboards. So, after finding the first one and thinking she'd solved the problem, the smell would only get worse from the second fish. And it did get worse. They didn't manage to find the second fish for weeks and Hughes had to move into another room.'

'Did Marie get caught?' I asked. 'They must have known it was her.'

'No, she got away with it. There were a few girls who cleaned the rooms, so she wasn't the only suspect. The nuns did call an assembly when they found the first fish, though. They gave us all a warning, but we didn't care by then. They punished Sally, which was predictable, and we'd already come up with a plan for that. When Sally stood outside in the courtyard, we'd set up a diversion elsewhere and then send someone else out to swap with her to give her a break. The person had to be a similar size, but with the hood of our tunics pulled over our heads and a scarf wrapped around our faces, we all looked the same. At the end of the punishment, when a nun shouted that you could come in, you'd simply walk back to the dorm. They never knew we did it.'

'Did you ever have to do it, Aunty Flo?'

'Yes, I did it. I did it twice. It wasn't very nice, but I was happy to do it for Sally, we all were. We just wished we'd done it sooner for Gertrude.'

'What else did the nuns say at the assembly?'

'I can't remember. They tried to scare us, but it was the best thing that could have happened because all of a sudden everyone knew about The Resistance, and they all wanted to join. That's when we had more recruits and we could have bigger meetings and come up with better ideas, and it was at the very next committee that we decided to fight fire with fire.

'We introduced a new rule. Whatever the nuns did to us, we would do it back to them. When they turned off the heating to our dorms, we'd turn off the heating to theirs. When we had icy cold showers in the mornings, we'd make sure they did too, and we now had Siobhan Docherty, who knew how to do it. She was a tomboy from the East End and her dad was a bit of a handyman, who could fix anything. He'd shown her how things worked, so she knew what pumps to break and what valves to turn off and what pipes to drain down, all that kind of thing. But before Siobhan went in, we'd have to send in our secret weapon first.'

'What was that? What was the secret weapon?' I asked, and I felt a tingle of excitement spill down my back.

'Clara Quinn. Clara Quinn was our secret weapon. Whenever we had to distract one of the gardeners or the maintenance men in the boiler house, we pointed her in the right direction, and she did the rest. She was a couple of years older, and she was pretty and had a big chest, and all the men fell over themselves when she walked by. They were a great team, those two; they did all the damage for us. If we wanted to give the nuns a cold shower, Clara unbuttoned the top of her blouse and dragged the boiler engineer off to the pantry, and Siobhan went in and turned off the hot-water valves. It was perfect.'

'The nuns must have been angry,' I said. 'What did they do next?'

'They knew they had a fight on their hands now, so they stepped it up a bit and they cut our food rations by half. Everything was exactly half, half for breakfast, half for lunch, half for dinner. Full rations were barely enough to live on, so when they halved it, we had a problem. We knew we had to come up with something. The committee meeting that night was the biggest one ever. The loft was crammed full of girls, and we hatched our plan. We decided on two things. To begin with, we would sabotage the nuns' food. If we were going to go hungry, then we would do everything we could to make sure they did, too. We arranged for the girls in the kitchen to drop stuff on the floor, and let the cat get at the food, things like that. And secondly, me and the other girls who worked in the house next door would smuggle in as much food as we could. Everyone at the house hated the nuns, and they knew full well what was going on, so they were only happy to help. They gave us a ton of food. We wrapped it in bags, and we stuffed it up our jumpers or strapped it to our legs, anything to get it back into the convent undetected. Everything we smuggled in got shared around as equally as possible. We agreed everyone would get the same amount, even those who'd refused to join The Resistance. But then it all went wrong.'

Aunty Flo broke off for a cigarette, but when she saw the "No Smoking" sign imprinted on the window, she muttered, 'Oh bollocks,' and slid the packet back into her bag.

'We had a blizzard that lasted for near on a week,' she continued, 'and the drivers couldn't get any deliveries through. The pantry stock had already run down, and we soon started running out of everything, so the nuns began to eat our food. Out of desperation, we tried to sneak in more food in from the house, but we took too many chances. Me and Anne McKinney got busted when the nuns searched us at the gate one day. Hughes went berserk. I've never seen anyone get so angry. We got sent up to our dorms and we knew a backlash was coming. A few minutes later, Radcliffe and Hughes burst into the dorm next to ours. We heard them scream, "You're all going to hell," and stuff like that. The next thing we knew, a girl got dragged out into the middle of the courtyard. They beat her with canes, but it wasn't a normal beating, it was something far worse. It was savage. And when they finished with that girl, they collected another and did the same. We called an emergency meeting, right there and then in the dorm, but nobody knew what to do. People were shouting to get the police or to tell the newspapers, but we'd already tried that months before. There was a war on, and nobody cared about a bunch of kids complaining about some nuns. Things got hysterical and everyone started arguing and blaming each other.

'All the other girls really went for the first seven of us. They said it was all our fault, but they especially blamed the leader, so in the end she lost her temper and stormed out to go down into the courtyard. When she got there, Hughes swung a cane at her, but she grabbed it and wrestled it away. Then she whacked Hughes around the side of the head. Radcliffe, who had been lashing the other girl, then got involved and, at the same time, most of the other nuns spilled out into the courtyard. That was it, we all went. Every single girl flew downstairs and flooded out into the snow, most of us without any shoes on. It made me think of a medieval battleground. The nuns were flailing their canes at us, but we easily outnumbered them and managed to snatch them away. A couple of the girls started battering Sister Holmes. She'd been pushed to the floor and a group of us had to calm those girls down before they went too far.'

The train shuddered to a stop in the middle of nowhere, and when Aunty Flo paused to look outside, I said impatiently, 'Tell me what happened then, Aunty Flo?'

'We cornered them. We drove all the nuns to the side of the courtyard. We told them they had to leave Sally alone and feed us properly and stop the beatings or we would do this again. We had them beaten. They knew it and there was this strange moment where nobody really knew quite what to do or say. In the end, some of the girls started drifting away and then we all went back to our dorms.'

'And then what happened?'

'That was it, really. When the snow had cleared, three bishops came in from somewhere and they took over for a bit while there was an inquiry. They interviewed all of us. We all told them about Gertrude, of which they clearly didn't know anything, and all the other things. We could tell they were shocked. We never saw Radcliffe again. Hughes stayed on, but she was a shadow of her former self after that. The nuns were still strict afterwards, but they never abused us again.'

The train pulled forward and started to gather pace, and Aunty Flo gazed out at the river below.

After some time, a question came to me, and I asked, 'Aunty Flo, who was she?'

'What do you mean?'

'Who was the leader? Who went down into the courtyard?'

'But, Jamie,' Aunty Flo replied with surprise, 'it was your nan. Your nan was our leader.'

The train slowed and arced around a curve, and I saw the sandstone spires of Oxford for the first time.

11

The train crawled into Oxford and lurched to a standstill. Heavy rain had been forecast for the weekend, and as we followed the crowd out of the station and passed a taxi rank, the first of it fell. I put up the umbrella and held it for both of us as we walked through the rain pelted puddles to a betting shop in Hollybush Row. Aunty Flo grinned when she emerged a few minutes later and said, 'Don't worry, we'll be back here later to collect,' and we promptly returned to the station for a taxi.

A black London cab sat at the front of the queue. Aunty Flo opened the back door and said, 'Donnington House, out on the Cheltenham Road,' and we climbed in as the old, grizzled driver folded his newspaper and grunted something back at her.

We pulled out into traffic, and I recalled the conversation I'd had with Aunty Flo the night before. She'd given me step-by-step instructions and to test my memory, I worked through each of them in sequence. As I did so, her mind must have gone back to the same conversation because she asked me, 'Are you alright, Jamie? And you know what you've got to do?'

'Yes, I'm OK thanks,' I replied. 'I know what to do.'

We inched out of town and the road eventually cleared after we'd crossed a large, elevated roundabout and exited onto a country road.

We drove for 20 minutes, the wipers squealing as they dragged across the windscreen. After taking a sharp bend and passing a series of dilapidated farm buildings, Aunty Flo said to the driver, 'Take this left, and then turn right at the junction.'

Fields of farmland passed on either side for miles until the road petered out into a single-lane track and the driver asked, 'Are you sure this is right, misuses?'

'Yep, keep going,' my aunt said. 'Another couple of miles from here and then it's on the left.'

A Cotswold stone wall appeared on my side of the car and when we reached a pair of iron gates, the driver turned in and stopped the car.

He began to say, 'What do we—' but before he had finished, the gates opened automatically.

Our tyres crunched over gravel as we drove down a long tree-lined driveway and over to my left, through the rain and the naked branches, I saw a grand brick-built manor house with steps leading up to an ornate entrance porch.

'Is that it?' I asked. 'Is that where we're going?'

'That's it,' Aunty Flo said, 'that's Donnington House.'

'It looks like it's haunted.'

Aunty Flo leant on my shoulder to see for herself and said, 'It is haunted.'

'What?'

'It's always been haunted, ever since it was built.'

'Are you joking?'

'No, it's true. There's a ghost. There always has been. They call him Little Bob.'

'Little Bob?'

'Yeah, he's famous around here. He was a young servant boy called Robert, probably not much older than you actually, and he lived here during the English Civil War. The Royalists killed him, and he's haunted the place ever since.'

'He was eleven and they killed him?'

'They hung him. He murdered three soldiers, so, to set an example, they executed him.'

'Is that definitely true?' I asked.

'Oh yeah, it's well documented. It's in history books and everything.'

'I can't believe they executed a young kid. How did he kill the soldiers?'

'He shot them. When the Royalists attacked the house, everyone else fled, but he got left behind for some reason and he wouldn't surrender. He found an old musket and he fired it at the soldiers from one of the windows up there. So, the soldiers held back and kept their distance and waited for nightfall, but by the time they'd managed to sneak in, he'd already escaped. He ran for miles until he found a barn to hide in, and he stayed there for a few days until the farmer saw him, and, thinking he'd get a reward, the farmer turned him in.'

The car swung into the courtyard in front of the house and pulled around a tiered water fountain.

'They hung him from one of the trees down by the lake,' Aunty Flo carried on, 'and ever since, he's stuck around to haunt the place.'

'What does he do?'

'Pull up just over there please, driver,' Aunty Flo said. 'Not many people have seen him, but everyone hears him all the time. He's always banging around upstairs at night and there's one bedroom nobody will go in because they say it's cursed.'

The car stopped outside the entrance. Aunty Flo paid the taxi driver and, after taking his number for our return journey, we stepped out into the pouring rain.

'Remember what I said, Jamie,' Aunty Flo said as we climbed the steps. 'There's nobody in hell today, the bastards are all here. We've got to watch each other's backs.'

An old man wearing a long black mourning suit with tufts of grey hair either side of a blotchy bald head dragged open the huge timber door and let us pass with a subtle bow and a muted smile.

The porch gave onto a crowded double-height entrance hall with a red-carpeted staircase, and the stairs climbed up to a gallery that wrapped around all four sides of the room. We hung our coats up in the cloakroom and then watched as butlers and waitresses carrying silver trays of drinks weaved through the mass of people dressed in black.

'Is this a hotel or do people live here?' I asked as I stared up at the glass chandelier.

'This is their house. They live here.'

We moved to the corner and Aunty Flo ran her finger across the top of a cast-iron radiator with flaking brown paint to find a layer of dust. 'They've let this place go downhill,' she said, as the heat pipes coughed and spluttered.

She picked up a sherry and an orange juice from a passing tray and after she'd handed me the juice, she sipped at the sherry and scoured the room for people she knew.

Before long, she caught the attention of a middle-aged man with blond floppy hair, who turned and eased his way through the crowd towards us.

'Well, well, Gillian,' he said icily, 'you did come after all. I really didn't think you'd have the nerve. Even by your standards, this really is quite something.'

I didn't know why he called Aunty Flo, Gillian, but I was more consumed with the way he spoke. I didn't like it. He gave me the impression he had something jammed up at the top of his mouth and, as a result, he had no choice but to force his words out of his thin pointy nose.

'Hello, Rupert,' Aunty Flo said in an equally frosty fashion. 'I've come to pay my respects to your father. That's what people do at funerals, isn't it? Pay their respects. Whatever you say about Sir Richard, I know he was a kind and decent man.'

'Oh, spare me, will you, for God's sake,' Rupert sneered. 'Have you really got to drag all that up today of all days? We've been through it so many times before. I'll never know why he favoured you, the poor little servant girl sent here to scrub the floors. Let me tell you something, something I've not told you before. He brought us up to be just like him. You know that? We were exactly as he intended us to be, until you came along with your accent and your jokes and that fucking smile of yours, and all of a sudden that's what he wanted from all of us. It makes me sick. But, and I'm certain you won't have forgotten this, the last time you were here he threw you out never to return, you remember that?'

'You know full well I didn't do anything that day,' Aunty Flo shot back, 'and he knew it too.'

'He had to decide, didn't he? It was either Consuela and I, or it was you. It was no more complicated than that. We gave him the opportunity and he made his decision. He chose his own children, his own flesh and blood. What is it you people say? Blood is thicker than water?'

'But you never forgave him, did you?' Aunty Flo said emphatically, and she let the question hang in the air with the murmur of the crowd.

Rupert looked away, and I saw his lips move as if he was rehearsing what to say next. He'd seen me when he first approached, but caught up in his rage at Aunty Flo, he hadn't thought to give me a second look.

As Rupert struggled for a reply, the bald man who greeted us at the door came over.

'Excuse me, Mr de Savery,' he said, 'it's almost time, sir.'

'Yes, very good,' Rupert snapped back. 'Give it ten minutes and then do the honours, will you, Sampson?'

Sampson went away and, without another word, Rupert followed.

Aunty Flo drained her sherry and swiftly plucked another from the tray of a smiling waitress.

'Wanker,' she said.

I let her drink her sherry and say 'wanker' twice more before asking her, 'Aunty Flo, why did he call you Gillian?'

'What an absolute wanker.'

'I know, but why did he call you Gillian?'

'What are you talking about?' she asked, as if I'd gone mad.

'He called you Gillian?'

'Yeah.'

'But why? Why did he call you Gillian?'

A woman with sharp features and short-black-straight hair barged through the crowd until she stood in front of us, arms folded but with one hand loose, casually holding what looked like a large whiskey or brandy. 'Hello, Gillian,' she said.

'Hello, Consuela.'

'Who are you?' she asked me abruptly as she put the glass to her thin, unmoving lips.

'Jamie,' I stuttered back.

'Really?' she replied. 'You're Jamie, Jamie Callaghan? Regan and Angela's boy? Well, well, if you've—'

Aunty Flo stepped half in front of me and said, 'You stay away from him.'

'Or what, Gillian?' Consuela said. 'What is it exactly that you're going to do?'

'Just—' Aunty Flo started, but she got cut short.

'You watch what you say when you're talking to me. Just remember, you're not talking to my halfwit brother now.'

Aunty Flo faltered.

'If I want to talk to Jamie,' Consuela said, swirling the drink around in her glass, 'then I will talk to Jamie.'

Aunty Flo mustered a reply. 'Just leave him alone. If you've got something to say, you say it to me.'

Consuela's response was instant and blunt. 'Alright, I will. Why are you here?'

'I've come—'

'You get nothing in the will, you must know that. You can't possibly think you're going to get something?'

'I've not come for that; I've come to pay my respects.'

Consuela laughed. 'Don't lie to me. You've come for something; I know you have. You wouldn't be here if you weren't here to get something, and why have you brought him? What are you up to?'

'He was a kind man and—'

'You won't get it. Whatever it is you've come for, you won't get it. I'll make sure of that.'

Sampson, who had positioned himself three or four treads up on the rising staircase, tapped a spoon against a glass to get people's attention. Consuela twisted around on her heels when she heard the noise. She turned back to us and said, 'I'm watching the pair of you,' and without waiting for an answer, she slipped away.

When the background noise had subsided, Sampson announced in a booming voice, 'Ladies and gentlemen, welcome to the funeral of Sir Richard de Savery, please proceed to St Mark's Chapel located in the Alexandra de Savery wing.'

Two seemingly identical corridors extended in either direction away from the entrance hall. We filed in behind the throng of people moving to our right, and, as we did so, I surveyed the empty corridor on my left that stretched down to the opposite end of the house.

As we shuffled along, I asked Aunty Flo, 'Are you OK?' and when she failed to respond I grabbed at her arm. 'Aunty Flo, are you alright?'

'Yes, yes I'm fine,' she replied, but I had my doubts.

When we entered the chapel, located down a short run of stairs at the end of the long corridor, a young woman in a black dress with a white lace collar held out a piece of paper for Aunty Flo. 'Service sheet for the ceremony, madame?'

Aunty Flo didn't reply.

I went to say something, but the young woman beat me to it. 'Excuse me, madame?' she repeated.

Aunty Flo came out of her stupor. 'Yes please, dear,' she said. 'Sorry. I'm miles away today.'

When she had taken the sheet of paper, we entered the chapel. We dropped into the back row, and I took in my surroundings as we nudged along to the rear corner.

I'd expected a straightforward room set out with lines of chairs, but the chapel was a full-size church, only slightly smaller than St Mary's in Thatcham, complete with stained-glass windows and rows of uncomfortable wooden pews.

At the front of the chapel, rain hammered down on the largest and most elaborate window, and immediately beneath it sat a lonely coffin resting on a plinth.

A vicar with wild, wiry, black hair entered through a side door behind the pulpit. He solemnly welcomed everybody, and we all stood up for the first hymn.

Most people sang but were drowned out by the elderly couple two rows in front of us who knew the words and sang heartily without the need of a service sheet.

Aunt Flo stared blankly at the words on the page.

As the couple sang of 'our Lord' and 'our Saviour' I wrestled with Consuela's stinging words and the size and scale of her house, which had a church built into it. Aunty Flo appeared to be reeling from Consuela's attack, and it had surprised and shaken me. Up until a few moments before, I'd had every confidence my aunt would dig me out of any kind of trouble if something went wrong, but now with that assurance drained away, I felt small and alone and in a world where I didn't belong.

'Please be seated,' the vicar said when the song had finished. He went on to describe Sir Richard's life, from growing up in Donnington House and going to university, to his time as chairman of a bank in Hong Kong, and finally his return to Oxford as a professor of economics.

I wondered who had written the words as the vicar read them out somewhat mechanically.

They listed Sir Richard's achievements but made no mention of his family and gave very little away about who he was and what his passions were.

The vicar then read out a prayer, and while he did so, I opened my eyes and leant to my right to see Consuela in the front row through the columns of bowed heads. Disinterested in the prayer, she glanced around disapprovingly at the people behind her and then down at her watch.

Another two hymns followed, sandwiched either side by a poem I found difficult to follow, and read out by Sir Richard's younger sister.

After the vicar's final prayer, he explained the burial would be a private family matter in the estate's grounds tomorrow, and he brought proceedings to a close. We waited for the chapel to empty before shuffling out into the corridor at the back of the group.

When we returned to the entrance hall, we found a buffet set out in front of six large circular tables, all surrounded by burgundy velvet chairs.

There weren't enough seats to go around and, as people realised some would be left standing, swarms of bodies busily descended upon chairs and tried to gather together into their groups. In amongst the chaotic scenes, Aunty Flo elbowed me and said, 'Now's your chance, Jamie. Go. Remember what I said, but you've got to be quick.'

I left her behind, worked my way through the muddle of mourners, and exited the hall to the opposite wing of the house. Flanked on either side by heavy panelled doors and portraits of past de Savery family members, I made my way down the long corridor.

'Where are you going?' a waiter carrying a tray of drinks asked me as I turned a corner.

'The toilets are busy down there, so I was sent up here. Where are they exactly?' I'd practised and perfected the line Aunty Flo had given me.

'Just a bit further down,' the waiter said after a doubtful pause, 'the gents' are on the right.'

I smiled innocently. 'Thank you.'

When the waiter had gone, I moved on past the toilets. I went through a door on my left into a dark library where walls of full-height bookshelves surrounded rows of reading tables, each with a green ceramic table lamp.

'Go to the bookcase in the far right corner,' Aunty Flo had repeated several times, 'and find the big blue book on the bottom row at the very end of the shelf.'

I ran diagonally across the carpet, weaving between the tables. In the far corner, I reached down, finding a worn and tatty blue hardback book. As instructed, I pulled it backwards. When the book had rocked back 45 degrees, I heard the click of a latching mechanism and I pushed the shelf backwards. It wouldn't budge at first, but when I pressed my shoulder against it, it gradually shifted. After three hard shoves, the bookshelf had scraped backwards on its hinges wide enough for me to slip in behind it.

I removed the pencil torch Aunty Flo had given me from my pocket, switched it on, and squeezed in behind the secret door. On the other side, I found steps leading down to a damp brick tunnel. I closed the door behind me and the lever release mechanism latched. When I faced the stairs and the way ahead, I realised Little Bob must have used this tunnel to make his escape. I shone the torch beam on the first step and went down, following in his footsteps.

12

At the bottom of the steps, I found a narrow brick tunnel that extended straight ahead into darkness. Water trickled away through drainage channels at the base of the walls and the air was dank and musty from a lack of ventilation.

For a moment I turned and stared up at the secret library door, but the thought of returning to Aunty Flo empty-handed and with nothing but feeble excuses drove me forward.

I wanted to sprint and get to the end of the tunnel as quickly as possible, but the weak light from my torch barely lit up more than a couple of metres in front of me, so I kept my pace at a slow walk.

I splashed through puddles and passed the rotting carcasses of dead rats as I travelled for what felt like miles, and it became clear the tunnel extended a considerable distance from the house.

When my torch did finally detect something up ahead, a wall seemed to close off my way out. But as I drew closer, and to my immense relief, I realised the wall simply led to a change of direction, and when I edged around the corner, I found a staircase rising to a door with chinks of light shining through.

At the top of the steps, I gratefully pushed open the door and drank in mouthfuls of fresh air. I'd emerged from a small enclosure shrouded in dense hedgerow and built in the same brick as Donnington House.

My eyes adjusted to the light and from what I could make out, the hedge, which extended in either direction, shielding me from any onlookers up in the windows of the house above, appeared to mark the boundary of the grounds.

The overgrown grass field in front of me stretched away before rising steeply into woodland and away to the west, beyond three grand oak trees, I saw the lake cloaked in a light mist. A rickety timber boathouse perched on the near side of the water, and I headed towards it.

I ran through the spitting rain and the long grass and when I passed under the overarching canopy of the nearest oak tree, I wondered whether Little Bob's young, lifeless body had once swung from one of its branches.

I went into the boathouse, out of the wet, and in the gloomy light I found two varnished timber speedboats rocking on the water. The gangways on either side were filled with wooden racks full of pots and jars and various tools hung from brackets on the walls, all precisely as Aunty Flo had described.

Her instructions took me upstairs to the upper floor, but that's where my memory failed me. In amongst the tables and chairs and an empty bar I imagined would be well stocked with bottles of gin and tonic come the summer, I couldn't remember where I had to go next. I scanned the floor, at first in a haphazard fashion, but then in a more methodical pattern, sweeping up and down the length of the room from one side to the other. In the second corner I inspected, I thought I'd located what I was looking for. I wriggled the loose floorboard from side to side, before prising it open with the tips of my fingers.

I found an empty floor void beneath, and I stared into it in disbelief. Two thoughts immediately came to mind: either I'd removed the wrong floorboard or somebody had already taken what I'd come for. Before resuming my search elsewhere, I stretched my arm into the void. I pulled out an empty cigar packet and a piece of paper that appeared to be a label from a pot of paint, and then when I stretched further, I touched upon something square and metal. My first attempt to claw it closer only managed to push it further away but, by extending my arm as far as it would reach, I managed to drag the metal container closer.

The flat metal tin I now found in front me was caked in a layer of dust and when I removed the lid, I picked out an unsealed envelope stuffed full of cream sheets of thick-cut paper.

'Get me those bits of paper, Jamie,' Aunty Flo had told me the night before. 'They're what it's all about.'

I swiftly removed the envelope, returned the empty tin to the void, and repositioned the loose floorboard.

Conscience of the time I'd been away, I rushed down the stairs with the envelope, but my progress was abruptly checked when I reached the door. A man in overalls and wellington boots, who I judged to be a groundsman for the estate, came striding toward me from the direction of the tunnel. He didn't see me, and I instinctively retreated into the boathouse, but once there, I quickly realised I'd be trapped if he came inside. I decided to take a chance. I darted outside and around to the blind side of the building.

The man came closer and shouted down towards the lake, 'Pete, is that you?'

I slid down the wall and crouched.

'Pete, Pete, are you down there?'

I waited and listened intently to the patter of rain on the roof. The next sound I heard came from inside the boathouse. The groundsman stomped up the stairs, stayed for an instant, and then came down.

In no time, he was back outside, his squelching boots coming closer to my side of the building. A few steps more and he would see me.

I had nowhere to go. The lake, pummelled by raindrops and gently lapping at the muddy embankment, blocked my escape.

At the front of the boathouse, I heard the groundskeeper mutter to himself, before he tramped away to join a path I suspected led up and around to the front of the house.

If he had turned, he would have seen me, now standing with my back to the wall like a prisoner waiting for the firing squad to pull the trigger. But he didn't, and when he was out of sight, I raced through the rain to the entrance of the tunnel. I descended and walked along it as fast as my dim torchlight would allow.

When I climbed up the steps to the secret door, the lever mechanism latched, and I pulled the door open more easily than I'd expected. The library remained as dark and empty as when I had left it.

Once inside, I shut the door and tucked the envelope under my shirt and jumper and into the front of my trousers.

I sped across the library to the men's toilets I'd passed on my way through. Squatting underneath it, I used the electric hand dryer to dry my hair and jumper. Looking into the mirror, I dragged my hair into position with my fingers and saw with some relief that my dark grey jumper, although still damp, didn't show it. Hoping not to bump into the same waiter as before, I went out into the corridor and followed the noise of the crowd to the entrance hall.

Most people had finished eating and were now either sat around the tables or stood in groups talking. I searched for Aunty Flo, but I couldn't place her.

Over my shoulder, I heard Consuela bark, 'Where have you been?' and I realised she was talking to me.

I spun around to find Aunty Flo next to her, holding a plate of food in one hand and a fork in the other.

'How's your tummy, Jamie?' Aunty Flo asked quickly. 'What is it, diarrhoea? Vomiting? Both?'

'Where have you been?' Consuela repeated.

'I've been in the toilet, I'm not feeling so great,' I said, rubbing my stomach and feeling the top of the envelope through my jumper as I did so.

'Alright, Jamie,' Aunty Flo said, 'we should get going. I'll call the taxi.'

'You can't go,' Consuela snapped. 'You've got to stay, Gillian.'

'No, we're going. Jamie's not well, so we'll be heading off.'

'You've got to stay for the reading of the will,' Consuela said, 'it's at 3pm.'

'No, I don't think we'll bother. You said yourself I'm no longer in it, so what's the point?'

'That's exactly the point. You've got to hear for yourself that you're not in it. I spoke to our lawyer earlier, and he said you absolutely must be there.'

Consuela eyed Aunty Flo's bag and then looked me up and down suspiciously before marching away. She found Sampson at the base of the staircase and spoke to him while they both looked over in our direction, and I guessed she was telling him to stop us if we tried to leave.

Aunty Flo put her plate down on the nearest table and moved us over to two chairs at the side of the room.

'Did you get the envelope?' she asked.

'Yes.'

'You did? You did get it?' she said with surprise.

'Yes, it's under my jumper.'

'Are you sure? You've definitely got it and it's all there?'

'I think so. The envelope's full up.'

'Well done, Jamie, well done,' she said excitedly.

'What are they?' I asked. 'What are the bits of paper?'

'They're bonds, banking bonds.'

'Yes, that's what it says on them, but what are they? What are they for?'

'It's like money. You can change them for money.'

'Do they belong to Consuela?' I asked and as I said it, I saw Consuela across the hall as she ignored the woman talking to her to glower in our direction.

'No, they're mine, but we can't let anyone know we've got them.'

'Why?'

'We just can't.'

'Why were they hidden here?'

'They were given to me when I was working here years ago, and I hid them to keep them safe. But when I had to leave in a hurry, I didn't get the chance to take them with me. They've been here ever since. I've not had the chance to come and get them until the funeral today gave me an excuse to come back.'

'Who gave them to you?'

'My Jack did.'

'Why did he have banking bonds?' I asked, and it felt as though every answer she gave needed two more questions.

'One of my friends wanted them.'

'Where did he get them?'

I got the impression Aunty Flo wasn't really concentrating on her replies, and I suspected she was desperate to see the bonds for herself.

'But, Aunty Flo,' I tried again, 'I don't get it. Why would Uncle Jack have banking bonds?'

'My Jack.' Aunty Flo sighed. 'He was bloody useless at everything apart from one thing. He could get hold of things. Whatever it was, if you asked him, he could lay his hands on it. It became a bit of a hobby of his and he did it all the time. I'd wake up in the morning and find all kinds of things in the flat.'

'So how exactly did he get them? What was his hobby?'

Aunty Flo looked at me as though I should know the answer, and she said, 'Armed robbery.'

Two elderly gentlemen, with white hair and rows of medals pinned on their blazers, strolled past squabbling about the England cricket team.

'Are they worth a lot?' I asked.

'I don't know exactly, but it'll be thousands of pounds.'
'Really? What will you spend it on?'
'Nothing, I don't need anything.'
'So, what will you do with them?'
'I'm giving them to you.'

I paused for a moment, shocked by her answer. 'Me? Why me?'

'Me and your nan decided you should have them. They're for when you're older, to help get you started out. They should grow in value the longer you have them and when you want to turn them into money, this is where you need to take them.'

She proceeded to tell me and went on to say she'd write down the address for me when we got home.

We sat on our chairs and watched the mourners slowly, one by one, say their goodbyes, collect their coats and leave as the clock gradually counted down towards 3pm.

By 2:50pm almost everybody had gone, and the staff began to clear away the tables. Rupert emerged from the corridor and beckoned Aunty Flo over.

'You'd better stay here,' Aunty Flo said to me. 'Keep those bonds safe.'

All of a sudden, I felt hungry, so I collected a plate and filled it with three sandwiches from the dozens that were left over. I returned to my seat in the corner and watched the staff clear away the glasses and dirty plates and then fold up the tables and wheel them down the corridor towards the library. With nothing else to do, I thought about the secret door and the tunnel and the oak trees and the loose floorboard and although everything had gone exactly to plan, I couldn't shake the aching doubt in my mind that something would yet go wrong. Sat hunched over on my chair, I could feel the envelope of bonds stuffed in my trousers and I knew that Consuela would undoubtedly take them from us and call the police if she knew we had them.

After not more than twenty minutes, Aunty Flo reappeared and tugged at my arm. 'Come on, we're off,' she said.

As she dragged me across the hall, I asked, 'Aren't you supposed to be in that meeting?'

'Consuela and the lawyer were arguing, so I told Rupert I needed the loo and slipped out. If we stay here, we're going to get busted. Consuela only wanted to keep us back so she could search us when everyone had gone. If we split now, we've got a chance. You've still got the bonds?'

'Yes, I've got them, but how are we going to get back to Oxford?'

'The taxi will meet us at the end of the drive. I used the phone in Sir Richard's old drawing room.'

As we approached the porch, I saw a butler stood in the doorway. It wasn't Sampson, who I assumed must be in the meeting, but a younger colleague who looked remarkably like him but with more hair.

When we ducked into the cloakroom to collect our coats, Aunty Flo said to me, 'Hold your stomach, pretend you're ill.'

'Stand back, dear,' Aunty Flo said to the younger version of Sampson as we bundled towards the door. I held my stomach and let out a pathetic groan as he tried to say something, but Aunty Flo talked over him.

'He's got the shits, dear,' she said, and she raised the palm of her outstretched arm so he'd keep his distance.

'You'd better stand back. It's not pretty and I think it might be catching. I'm not feeling too great myself.'

We went out the door and down the steps, but instead of walking across the courtyard, Aunty Flo dragged me over a lawn that led into the woods.

As we trampled over a carpet of brown soggy leaves, I said to Aunty Flo, 'Will they come after us when they realise we've gone?'

'They might do,' she replied, glancing over her shoulder. 'I told the taxi to get a move on and we'll cut through here to join the drive further up to save time.'

'Do you want to see the bonds?' I asked.

'No, keep them stashed.'

'But you've waited all this time for them, don't you want to see them?'

'No, not really,' she said dismissively.

We climbed out from the woods and joined the driveway when the entrance gates were in sight. The gates were open.

'What's that noise?' I asked.

We both stopped and faced down the gravel drive towards the house.

I heard it again, unmistakable this time: the sound of barking dogs. Through the woods, in the distance and in the direction we had just come from, we saw a gang of men with five Dobermanns on leads charging towards us. They must have seen us at the same time. We heard a roar go up and the dogs were cut loose.

'We need to get out of here,' Aunty Flo cried, but before we had turned, we saw a pick-up truck turn from the courtyard and start hurtling down the driveway in our direction.

'Run, Aunty Flo,' I shouted.

I ran ahead for the gates, praying they wouldn't close on me before we got there. Judging by the rate the dogs and the truck were closing in, our only hope was for the taxi to be there waiting and even then, I wasn't sure if Aunty Flo would make it. She ran as fast as she could with her handbag flailing, but her top speed was agonisingly slow.

'Come on, Aunty Flo!' I screamed.

Running as fast as I could, I thought ahead as the gates approached. When I found the taxi at the end of the road, I would ask him to turn into the driveway and pick up Aunty Flo.

When I reached the entrance, I looked up and down the road to see where the taxi had parked. It wasn't there. It hadn't arrived yet. I stood there helplessly, not knowing what to do.

The next thought that came to me, was that of the Dobermann dogs mauling Aunty Flo. I raced back to her.

She'd covered more ground than I had thought she would, but the dogs and the truck were closing in fast.

'The taxi's not here! We're not gonna make it.'

'Just keep going,' she cried while struggling to catch her breath, but it was clear to me we had nowhere to go.

When we arrived at the gates, I saw, far off in the distance, our taxi sweeping slowly around a bend. 'The taxi's coming,' I said breathlessly, 'but it's too far away. They'll get us before it gets here.'

Aunty Flo, wheezing heavily, positioned herself by the post at the side of the entrance gates.

In a ditch by the side of the road, I found a broken-off branch. I picked it up. It would at least provide some sort of defence against the dogs when they got to us.

I went over to Aunty Flo, who had her back to me. I could clearly see and hear the five Dobermanns coming now. The pick-up truck still had some ground to cover, and I realised we'd have to defend ourselves from the dogs for some time before it got to us.

Out of desperation, I looked towards the taxi, but it was still too far away and the noise of dogs barking drew ever closer.

'I've got this,' I said to Aunty Flo, and I held up the stick, preparing to defend her with it.

'Stand back,' she said.

'What are you doing?' I asked. When I peered around her, I saw she had unscrewed the fascia of the control panel on the gate post with her nail file. She reached in to grab the exposed cables, turned her head, and then yanked them out of their terminals. Sparks flew from the box and the gates began to close.

'Bingo!' Aunty Flo cried out.

The gates closed tight, and we stood there, relieved. The five Dobermanns arrived and furiously jumped up to bark and paw and scratch at the gates.

'That was close,' I said. 'How did you know to do that?'

'A little trick my Jack once taught me,' Aunty Flo replied, and she ruffled my hair.

She linked her arm through mine, and we scurried along the road, leaving the noise of the dogs and the pick-up truck and the gang of men behind us until we drew alongside the taxi, and it picked us up.

After Aunty Flo and the taxi driver had exchanged the usual pleasantries, she sank back in her seat and puffed out her cheeks.

The taxi negotiated the winding country roads and turned onto the main road to Oxford. As we sped along, I took out the envelope stuffed with banking bonds and gave it to Aunty Flo, who slid them into her bag.

I watched the side of her face for a few moments, and I then asked her, 'Would you have gone to the funeral today if the bonds hadn't been there?'

'Definitely,' she said. 'I wouldn't have missed it for the world.'

'But Consuela said you only went there to get something else?'

'Don't listen to her. She doesn't know anything. Sir Richard was kind to me at a time when I was surrounded by nothing but cruelty. Believe me, that is not something you forget in a hurry. I'll always be grateful for that. I was thinking about it earlier actually, when we were in the chapel. There's one memory in particular that got stuck in my mind. Do you want me to tell you?'

'Yes, please.'

'We were down by the lake, where you went earlier, but the weather wasn't like this; it was beautiful, a glorious summer's day, and Sir Richard had been out on his boat with friends while I worked in bar. When he got back, he told me to fix us all a drink and then join him for a chat. It wasn't long after Jack had got pinched for one of his robberies and Sir Richard had kindly put up the bail money for me. I was trying to work out what to do. Should I stick by Jack or leave him for someone a bit more responsible? I was expecting Sir Richard to give me a bit of a lecture, but all he said was, "Do you love him? Nothing else matters. If you love him, then you'll know what to do." So that was it,

I decided there and then. Me and Jack got married two years later, after he got out.'

'When did Uncle Jack die?' I asked.

'Oh, it was years ago. Conor was only three when he died. The poor sod, for all his faults, he didn't deserve that; he didn't deserve to die so young. That's another thing Sir Richard did for me, now I think of it. A few years later, I was back in London and he contacted me out of the blue. He'd heard Jack was sick and he paid for him to go up Harley Street and see this top surgeon he knew. As it happens, it was too late and they couldn't do anything, but it did give us some hope for a while at least. I still don't even know how Sir Richard found out that Jack was ill. And then he came to the funeral. I didn't expect him to, but he did. He wanted to be there for me. I had to laugh. There he was in the Assembly House afterwards, a knight of the realm stood at the bar surrounded by half of London's worst criminals and villains. The funny thing is, he fitted in, and they all thought the world of him. "I'm a banker," he said to me, as he jostled at the bar and knocked back pints of lager, "I'm the biggest crook in here."'

I'd taken great pleasure from Aunty Flo's jubilant mood as we escaped from Donnington House, but now, as she told her stories, and contemplated Jack's and Sir Richard's lives, I lost her to a deep melancholy. For a long while, she stared out the window at the passing hedgerows and waterlogged fields before she finally said, 'It's my name.'

We turned to face each other at the same time.

'It's my name,' she repeated. 'Gillian is my name, my real name, but I've never liked it, so everyone calls me Florence. Well, nearly everyone; that lot back there call me Gillian because they know I don't like it.'

'I quite like Gillian,' I said, 'but I do prefer Florence. Aunty Flo, can I have permission to swear?'

'No, you can't.'

'Oh, come on, let me,' I pleaded.

'Why?'

'I need to, just this once. Please?'

'Alright, go on then, but don't tell your nan.'

'Thanks.'

'Go on then, say it.'

'That Rupert really is a wanker.'

Aunty Flo laughed. 'Well, Jamie, I think you might be right there.'

The car crossed the large roundabout and turned off towards the city centre. After fighting through the Friday-afternoon traffic, we arrived in Holybush Lane.

Aunty Flo leant forward and paid the taxi driver and, as she went to open the door, I asked her, 'Do you think your horses won?'

She grinned and said, 'Of course they did.'

At times, her eyes literally sparkled, and they did so now, when she said to me, 'Come on, Jamie, let's go and collect our winnings.'

13

Nan gave up her job at The White Hart the day Neil moved in.

When she quit, she told the landlord she'd be happy to help out with the odd shift if they ever needed cover. A fortnight later, he took her up on the offer and she agreed to work a Friday while he whisked his wife away to the Lake District for the weekend.

'Isn't that when everyone is coming down for my birthday?' I asked when she told me.

'That's right, love. They're all going down the pub and then we'll all come back here afterwards.'

'Are all your brothers and sisters coming?'

'Most of them. Alan and Barbara can't make it, but the rest of them will be there. You can bike up to meet us after school.'

When the day came, it was cold and crisp for most of the afternoon, but by the time I walked into the thick, smoky atmosphere of the pub, the blue winter sky had faded to a pink sunset.

I found the saloon bar empty, except for a pair of elderly women sat in the bay window playing cards, and a small group of people milling around at the bar.

A young barman prodded at the embers of the fire with a wrought-iron poker before using a pair of tongs to add lumps of coal from the scuttle.

I hung up my jacket. I couldn't see Nan, but I saw the back of Aunty Flo at the bar talking to two men. I tugged at her sleeve, but she didn't notice and carried on with her story.

'He was a bloody pervert. So, I told him to "fuck off" and when I turned around, who was standing there? It was only Princess Margaret with the bloody Queen!'

The two men burst out laughing.

I went to pull at my aunt's blouse again but, bitten by curiosity, I waited to hear what else she had to say.

'They'd come to look at a young foal they were thinking of racing,' she carried on. 'Princess Margaret couldn't stop laughing as she walked down the stables towards me. That bloody pervert had ducked out the back door as soon as he'd seen them, so I was all alone by the time they got to me.'

'What did you say?' the man smoking a cigar asked.

'What could I say?' Aunty Flo replied. 'I curtsied to the Queen and said, "Please excuse me, Your Majesty," and do you know what she said to me? "Good for you, Gillian, I would have done the same." And then Princess Margaret chipped in, "Yes, Gilly, well done but you should really have kneed him in the balls as well."'

The taller man leaning on the bar tossed his head back when he laughed, and his friend with the cigar choked a little as he chuckled.

Aunty Flo sensed me at her side and turned. 'Hello, Jamie, dear.'

She kissed my forehead. 'Your nan's in the other bar. How's your birthday so far?'

'Good, thanks. Aunty Flo, is that true? Have you really met the Queen?'

'Yeah, a few times. I worked at a stable where she used to visit every now and again.'

'You've never said anything before?'

'No, I guess not. I didn't think you'd be interested.'

'Was she nice?'

'She's alright,' Aunty Flo said, as if she was talking about a woman she met on the bus. 'I'll tell you one thing about her, that woman knows her horses. When she had the time, we'd talk for hours about them. She worked with all the world's top trainers, and she would tell me all the things they taught her about diet and breeding and preparation. Yeah, she was really nice when I think about it, but I knew Princess Margaret better though. She came over to the stables every week for a time when the Queen was off doing Queen stuff. We'd play gin rummy, and she'd bring some brandy, and it would be the decent stuff from the palace, not the usual cheap rubbish we used to get. She was a lot of fun. She'd tell more dirty jokes than all the stable lads put together. Much too rude for you, dear, but I expect these two would enjoy them.'

With her thumb, she gestured to the two men who were still listening.

'Come on, let's go and see your nan,' she said, and she pushed through a varnished wooden door with 'The Lounge Bar' etched into the frosted glass panel.

In among the bustling crowd, Uncle Pat saw me and said, 'Here he is; hello, Jamie.'

As he strode towards me, I saw Nan behind the bar, pulling a pint and laughing with her older sister, Mary.

Neil and Larry stood propped up against the bar chatting with Uncle Bill, and half hidden behind Larry, I picked out Freya, still wearing her school uniform.

Her fringe had been trimmed and her wide-open brown eyes held my gaze through the cigarette smoke. I'd barely seen her since our day together at Larry's. We'd exchanged the odd friendly glance as we passed in the corridor, but from what I could gather, she'd been off sick for most of the last three weeks.

Uncle Pat gave me a playful slap on the back. He had the same smile as Nan and Aunty Flo, and he beamed and said, 'Happy birthday, Jamie.'

'Your Aunty Florence dragged you along to that game last week, didn't she?' he said. 'Dear oh dear, that team of yours, what a load of rubbish.' He laughed and spilled his pint down his jumper before recovering to drink half of it.

'We played quite well,' I protested, determined to put up a bit of a fight, 'and we almost got a draw.'

'Almost got a draw? You lost three-nil? And from what I heard, you were lucky to get nil.' He laughed again and patted his stomach.

He winked at me, leant in, and put his hand on my shoulder. He knew Aunty Flo, who was standing over his shoulder talking to his wife Beryl, could hear him.

'I tell you what,' he said in a serious voice. 'You tell that aunty of yours you want to go to football with me instead. You tell her you want to go and see a decent team for once.'

'I heard that, Patrick,' Aunty Flo said, and she gave her brother a shove. 'You leave that boy alone.'

'I'll never change teams, Uncle Pat,' I said, playing my part. 'And we beat you last season one-nil.'

'But we've beaten you twice since then,' he said. 'You know what, I still can't believe my little sister Florence supports that team of yours. When we were kids, our dad, your great-grandad, he used to take all of us up the football on a Saturday. We'd all walk up to the stadium together. The whole family would go; even your nan came along in those days when she was a kid before she met your grandad, and we had so much fun together.'

'Here we go,' Aunty Flo said, rolling her eyes.

'Our dad would pay for us to get in the ground early,' Uncle Pat went on. 'And then he'd clear off up the pub with his mates, so we had the terraces to ourselves for a while. We'd play tag and race up and down the stands until the crowd turned in, and we'd go to our usual position in the north stand. I still stand there now, you know. And what a team we had in those days, we beat everyone. We saw some fantastic matches. But your Aunty Florence, she wouldn't come with us. No matter what we said to her, we couldn't get her to come. She'd stay at home by herself and listen to the horses on the radio. And then the next Saturday, when your lot were at home, she'd catch the bus up there by herself and watch them lose. They were just as rubbish in those days as they are now.'

He gave me a friendly cuff on the shoulder.

'You should have supported our lot, really,' he carried on. 'I can't believe how that aunt of yours got you to support them.'

A pang of anguish flashed across his face the moment he said it. He'd remembered that they were my dad's team, and he must have realised, a fraction too late, how easy it would have been for Aunty Flo to convince me.

I didn't want him to feel bad, and I said as cheerfully as I could, 'She can be very persuasive.'

'She can indeed,' he agreed, and I could tell that he wanted to make amends. 'I must admit that new striker of yours does look good. He'll score plenty of goals for you if he stays fit. We tried to buy him a couple of seasons ago, you know?'

'He did play well last week,' I said, 'until he limped off injured.'

He finished his drink. 'I tell you what, you're playing at our place next month. Why don't you and your nan and Flo come up to ours the night before for a little party? I'll get the others to come along as well, and then we'll walk up to the stadium together the following day. How does that sound?'

'That would be great, thanks, Uncle Pat. And we might beat you again?'

'We'll see about that.' He laughed. 'Right, I need another drink. What do you want? A Coke and a packet of crisps?'

I thanked him and worked my way through the crowd, accepting birthday wishes from uncles and aunts and cousins, and Aunty Mary stepped behind the bar so Nan could greet me.

'Hello, love,' she said. 'I hope you've had a nice day at school. We've closed this bar to the public so we could have a little party for you. I thought it was better to have it here rather than at home. That way we could get everybody to come.'

Her eyes diverted to Freya, who had moved with Larry and Neil to sit in the raised section at the rear of the pub.

'We'll bring out the food in a bit,' Nan said, 'and I've baked a couple of birthday cakes for you. They're over there on that table. We'll cut the cake after the food and then get the music turned up a bit. Is that alright, love?'

'Thanks, Nan.'

She must have seen my eyes flitting to the back of the room.

'I'm going to go and help out at the bar,' she said. 'Why don't you go and talk to her?'

On my way to see Freya, Uncle Pat intercepted me on the short run of stairs to the upper section.

'Here's your drink, Jamie,' he boomed. 'And I got a few packets for you all.' He grinned at Freya and threw the crisps on the table. 'How you doing, Larry?' he said. 'And you must be Neil—'

I pulled up a chair next to Freya and she wished me a happy birthday.

'Thanks for coming,' I said. 'I didn't expect to see you here.'

'Your nan knocked on my door on Tuesday afternoon,' Freya said, 'after my dad had left for his night shift. She asked me to come but said to keep it a secret from you so it would be a surprise.'

'But your dad doesn't know you're here, does he?'

'No, he thinks I'm at Carrie's birthday party. Your nan knows her mum and she agreed to cover for me.'

'That's good. I'm glad you came. And it gave you a chance to meet Neil.'

'Yes, he's really nice. He picked me up from Carrie's

in his van and I was talking to him and Larry before you arrived.'

At my back, I heard Uncle Pat say to Neil, 'What? Rugby?'

'Your aunty seems to take care of Neil,' Freya said. 'Apparently, she inspected him before he left and she made him change his shirt. He'd spilled baked beans all down it.'

I said, 'I've not seen you at school much. Have you been sick?'

'Yes, I've been a bit poorly.'

'Are you feeling better now?'

'I'm fine now, thanks,' she said, but she didn't convince me.

I wanted to ask her what had been wrong, but before I had a chance, Freya said, 'You have a nice family.' She sat forward in her chair to get a better look at the crowd. 'They all look similar, don't they? Your nan's brothers and sisters, they've all got the same laugh, and they all wear the same glasses.'

'There were 13 of them,' I explained. 'Apart from Aunty Sheila, Nan is the youngest and Aunty Flo is next. They had a brother, Peter, but he died when he was three and the eldest, Arthur, died two years ago. They're all getting quite old now, but they still like to get together for a party.'

'Are they all here?'

'Most of them. Alan and Barbara couldn't make it, and Sid moved to Boston in America a long time ago, so we don't see him very often, but apart from that, they're all here.'

Something caught Freya's eye. 'I think your Aunty Flo's had a bit too much to drink,' she said.

Aunty Flo staggered slightly to her right and felt for the banister on the stairs to steady herself.

'Are you alright, Aunty Flo?' I asked.

'Yes, dear.' She leant on the handrail and raised a smile. 'That brandy's gone to my head.' She checked up on Neil, who was still talking with Pat, and then said, 'I'll spend a penny and then I'll be back to talk to you two.'

She stumbled into the fire escape door, laughed at herself, and went upstairs to the toilets.

'Jamie, I need to talk to you,' Freya said, and something in her voice alarmed me.

'What is it? What's wrong?'

'You've got to be careful, not just you, but all of you.'

'But why? What's wrong?'

'I can't say, but you've got to be careful. Especially your nan.'

'Why? I don't understand. What do you mean? Be careful of what?'

Freya hesitated. She was breathing heavily.

'Please tell me,' I said. I wanted her to tell me and tell me quickly in the hope I could just as quickly dismiss it as nothing to worry about.

'Please,' I repeated, and she appeared to relent.

She shuffled her chair closer to mine. Whatever it was she had to say, she wanted to whisper it.

I dipped my head to listen but pulled up sharply.

The noise from the staircase brought the bar to silence. Two loud thuds in quick succession followed by a final sickening slap.

I raced to the escape stairs and got there first, ahead of Neil. I tugged at the door to open it. When it was ajar,

Neil grabbed the handle and forcefully dragged it wide open.

Aunty Flo lay face down on the tiled floor at the foot of the stairs.

She'd fallen with her left arm twisted underneath her body. At any moment, I expected her to shift into a more comfortable position, but she didn't move.

Nan fought her way through the crowd and brushed past me. She dropped to her knees. Over Aunty Flo's lifeless body, she screamed, 'Get an ambulance!'

Somebody, I think it was Sita, shouted back that she would go.

Neil propped the staircase door open with his foot. Through the opening, all eyes fixed on the two sisters.

Nan caressed Aunty Flo's hair and delicately drew it back to reveal her face, which was now contorted down the left side, with her eye and mouth drooping to break the symmetry.

'Please, Gilly, please don't go.' Nan wept and her body anxiously rocked back and forth as she knelt over. She continued to stroke Aunty Flo's hair, but then she stopped, pressed her head against her sister's and gently kissed her forehead. 'Please come back to me,' she pleaded. 'Please come back.'

A voice at the back of the crowd shouted, 'The ambulance will be ten minutes!'

Neil's hand trembled as it pressed up against the door. I sensed his face above me, but I couldn't bring myself to look at him.

Larry put his arm around me and pulled me in tight to his chest.

I was the first to speak. I asked, 'Nan, is she dead?'

14

SOMEWHERE IN BELGIUM, 1944

The German soldier in the barn rushed at Baxter with a knife.

Callaghan pulled the revolver from the holster on his belt. With no time to aim, he shot speculatively. The bullet caught the upper right side of the soldier's torso, twisting him around as he advanced.

Baxter had both his Sten and Enfield rifle straps over the same shoulder. He fumbled for the Sten, but the rifle came loose first, and he drove its butt into the German's face, knocking him forcefully backwards and to the ground.

Callaghan replaced his handgun, grabbed the rifle off his back and turned to the circle of soldiers. One of them, front and centre, who appeared to be a similar age to Callaghan, and whose face and hair were splattered with dried mud, had picked up a carbine from the floor. Callaghan quickly latched the safety, raised the rifle to this right eye and pulled the trigger to shoot the soldier in the chest.

Callaghan heard a second shot, and he knew Baxter had turned his rifle and killed his attacker.

An older German soldier at the back of the group, with cropped blond hair and wearing an untucked khaki shirt, got up to run. Callaghan's first shot missed, but his second caught him square in the ear and his limp body skidded to the ground.

A sharp movement to Callaghan's right caught his attention. He saw, too late, a young soldier in a helmet lining up a rifle at him. Before Callaghan had a chance to swing his gun around, a hail of bullets cut across the young man's midriff, and his body folded as it fell forward, with the discharge from his rifle blasting into the soil.

Baxter had thrown down the Enfield and unloaded the Sten. He shot from the hip and its rapid fire of shells pelted four of the remaining five men, making their bodies jerk awkwardly in different directions as the bullets tore into flesh.

One of the soldiers had managed to scramble away from the circle and escape behind a timber shack. Callaghan ran after him, and at the corner of the shack, he had a clean shot. He took aim, his first attempt hitting the fleeing German at the top of the left arm. Callaghan's second shot struck the centre of the soldier's spine, and he arched backwards, with arms flung open, before tumbling over.

Callaghan returned to the courtyard. 'Let's go,' he said hastily, 'there could be more of them.'

The cooking pot simmered over the dying fire as the two Englishmen picked their way through the dead bodies to exit out of the northern side of the courtyard.

They moved quickly and passed a whitewashed

farmhouse building. The house had broken windows and faced out onto an oval duck pond. A track ran away from the house and they followed it out of the farm.

After walking for an hour, Baxter asked, 'Can we stop for a rest, Bill?'

'Yes,' Callaghan agreed, 'but let's get up by that wall first.'

When the two men reached the crumbling dry-stone wall that ran down a gentle gradient to meet with the road, they eased off their rucksacks and flopped down on the grass.

Callaghan laid out flat with his head resting on his backpack. 'I'm not hungry now,' he said, and he felt his arms and fingers tingle as adrenaline coursed through his body.

Baxter, who sat cross legged and holding his water canister, replied with a shake of the head, 'No, me neither.'

After a long period of silence, Baxter took a gulp of water and asked, 'So you think you'll marry Betty when you get home, Bill?'

The question took Callaghan by surprise, but he welcomed the distraction, and he sat forward to answer. 'That's the plan,' he said. 'I'll get a job on the buses, and we'll get married and then try to find a little house somewhere.'

'In London?'

'I expect so. I can't see us ever leaving.'

'What about kids? Do you think you'll have children?'

'We want them,' Callaghan said. 'We talk about it all the time. Betty's desperate for a family. Me too. I think it's all we've ever wanted, really, a family of our own. Hopefully we'll have a few kids and do all the things that families do; take them down the coast and watch them play on the beach, that kind of thing.'

'That sounds nice.'

'What about you, Bax?' Callaghan asked. 'Have you got anyone at home? You've never said anything?'

'There is this girl,' Baxter said, taking another drink, 'her name's Mary, but I'm not sure if she'll marry me. I've asked her to come dancing with me a few times, but she's never been all that keen. Maybe I'll try again when I get home. You never know, things might be different after the war.'

'Where did you meet her?'

'At the post office; she works in the depot so I see her every morning. What about you and Betty? How did you two meet?'

'We've known each other for years. We went to the same school and our dads know each other. They drink in the same pub and go to football together. I guess I've always liked her, if I think about it, ever since we were kids. She was the girl at school all the boys wanted to go out with, but I didn't have the guts to go and speak to her back then.'

Callaghan brought his knees up and wrapped his arms around them. 'At the start of the Blitz she got sent out to a convent, so I didn't see her for a couple of years, but last year when she turned 16, she came back to London and started work at the war office. That's when I got a chance to see her again, when our families met up in the evenings in our dads' pub. I chickened out a couple of times, but in the end, I got up the courage to ask her out.'

The droning noise of a far-off engine interrupted Callaghan. He got up to find a single fighter plane with a white star on its fuselage, set against a clear blue sky and flying from north to south.

'It's one of ours?' Baxter asked.

'Yes, American. It looks like a Mustang.'

The plane disappeared out of sight and the hum subsided.

Callaghan grabbed the strap of his backpack. 'Let's get going, we'll stay off the road but we'll follow it up until we find Major Turnbull's group.'

The pair vaulted the stone wall and started out across the gently rolling landscape.

'Tell me more about your repair shop, Bax?' Callaghan asked.

'My watch mender's shop?'

'That's right, you started telling me about it as we came out of Normandy.'

'I've made up my mind,' Baxter said. 'I'm definitely going to do it. Lots of people bring me their watches so I've already got quite a few customers, and sometimes people have to wait for a couple of weeks, so if I did it full time, I could keep up a bit better.'

'And you're sure you want to leave the Post Office?'

'Yes. I'll try one more time with Mary, but even if she says yes, there's no reason for me to stay there. I've always been interested in repairing things, so I might as well do it as a job.'

'Will you get a little shop?'

'One day, maybe,' Baxter said, running the back of his arm across his forehead to clear away the sweat, 'but at first I'll just do it from home.'

'I'll make sure I bring my watch out to you when it packs up,' Callaghan said, and he gave Baxter a friendly slap on the top of his shoulder.

'I'd like that, Bill. You'd be welcome any time. There's a nice little pub down by the railway that I sometimes go to, I think you'd like it there.'

'OK, you're on,' Callaghan said.

After the two soldiers had walked late into the afternoon, Callaghan studied the landscape ahead, which had become more rugged and interspersed with dense clusters of majestic beech trees, and he took hold of his rifle.

'What's wrong, Bill?' Baxter asked.

'It's all these trees blocking our view,' Callaghan replied. 'If we stumble across that retreat, I'd like to see it from a safe distance.'

Baxter clutched his Sten, and they entered a strip of woodland that swept up from the road and continued to a steep ridge high up on their left.

The canopy of leaves overhead, which were still green and had yet to turn, blocked out all but the slightest glimmer of sunlight. They walked through bracken and over the occasional twig that snapped underfoot until Baxter felt for Callaghan's shoulder.

'Bill, through there,' he whispered, and he motioned to a large clearing in the trees up ahead.

Callaghan saw the tail fin first, slanting upwards at an odd angle and painted dark green and emblazoned with a black swastika.

As he moved forward to the edge of the trees, he noticed the scorch marks striped across the grassy glade and he realised the Luftwaffe fighter must have crash-landed. The engine and front end of the fuselage had burnt through, and the plane sat lopsided on its belly where its wheels hadn't opened out.

'Looks like it's been there a while,' Baxter said. 'What is it, a Focke?'

'No, it's a Messerschmitt,' Callaghan replied. 'A Bf 109. I've never seen one up this close before.'

Baxter's eyes anxiously darted around the glade. 'What do you think? Should we go around?'

'I just want to take a quick look,' Callaghan said.

'But why? We can go around.'

'I'll only be a couple of minutes.'

'Are you sure?'

'Yes, it'll be fine. You stay here, keep an eye out.'

Baxter lifted the Enfield and Sten straps from his shoulder. 'Be careful,' he said.

Callaghan edged out into the knee-length grass with his revolver ready. When he turned, he saw Baxter surveying the clearing down the barrel of his rifle.

The Messerschmitt sat tilted towards Callaghan, and as he approached, he saw the dead pilot in the cockpit. Judging by the charred propeller and paintwork, he reasoned the engine had been shot up and caught fire mid-air and either the pilot had been shot dead or he hadn't been able to bail out.

The grass swayed in the gentle breeze.

Callaghan stepped up on the wing and kicked away fragments of glass before sliding the revolver into his belt.

He tried to open the glazed cockpit canopy. It wouldn't shift at first, but Callaghan finally managed to flip it open.

He glanced back at Baxter, who remained vigilantly in position, his Enfield rifle scanning for danger.

Callaghan reached for his knife.

15

THATCHAM, ENGLAND, 1986

The 3:42pm London train pulled out of Thatcham station on time.

I sat in an empty carriage until Midgham, when an elderly couple came on board and joined me to sit two rows down.

The man moaned about his bad back until the ticket inspector came around when, after buying two old-age pensioner return tickets to Reading, he complained about the price of the tickets.

I paid for my ticket with what was left of the money Larry had given me, and after the inspector had moved to the next car, the old man reverted to complaints of his bad back.

The couple alighted at Reading as expected, and four schoolgirls with boater hats and matching yellow-and-burgundy blazers stepped on.

In the vestibule, one of the girls said, 'Let's sit here.'

She pointed to the seats opposite me, but the others looked down at the badge on my school jumper and dragged her in the opposite direction.

We spent six minutes parked at the station. Various announcements came over the loudspeaker and a herd of people on the adjacent platform hurriedly migrated to the stairs following a change of platform for the Plymouth train.

As the last of the stragglers shuffled onto the staircase, I removed a London A to Z map from my school bag and opened it on the scratched and graffitied table in front of me.

I'd secretly taken the map from Neil's van the night before. I knew he had work in Basingstoke all week so he wouldn't miss it.

The train eased out of the station, passing Reading prison.

I flicked through the well-used pages and found the address Aunty Flo had given me on our journey back from Oxford.

'Be careful around there,' I remembered her saying to me, 'the streets are crawling with weirdos and nasty bastards.'

I scanned the page for the nearest tube station and used the underground map on the back page to work out which line to take.

After memorising the route and road names I had to navigate on foot from the underground, I closed the book and stuffed it in my bag.

We arrived at Paddington Station at 4:35pm.

I made my way to the Bakerloo line and took the southbound train to Piccadilly Circus.

Darkness had fallen by the time I surfaced, but the

streets were illuminated by the brightly lit advertisements for American burger chains, Australian lager, and Japanese electronics.

A balding man in a grey trench coat stopped and asked, 'Are you looking for me?'

When I realised he was talking to me I said, 'No,' firmly and moved away.

I'd chosen the wrong subway exit and found myself on the south side of Piccadilly Circus.

To head north, I weaved through the stationary traffic on Piccadilly and as I stepped behind a bus, I breathed in the smell of pungent petrol fumes.

When I reached the wide, sweeping pavement on the north side of Regent Street, it was full of smiling foreign tourists with cameras and serious-looking businessmen and women marching in long black coats.

A headwind gathered. I drove forward against it and around the curve until the road straightened and I saw Glasshouse Street over to the right.

I crossed the road, skipping between the double-decker buses and black taxis, and I left the grand Regency boulevard behind for the back streets of Soho.

Aunty Flo's warning came back to me.

To secure my bag, I lifted the strap over my head so it crossed my chest diagonally and I pulled it around to the front so I could keep my hands on it.

Outside a noisy pub, I went over to the south side of Glasshouse Street to avoid a tramp writhing in sodden blankets, but the smell of urine followed me across the road.

Further down, as Glasshouse Street forked left into Brewer Street, I saw the address I'd come for. The entrance was two doors along from a peep show with a "Girls, Girls, Girls" sign and pictures of women in black silhouette, mounted on a filthy mirrored front window.

Two women in tatty fur coats appeared at the peep show door. I twisted awkwardly away from them as they shouted over, 'Hello, sonny, come and talk to us; you got any money?'

A sign above the entrance doorway read "Roxy's" in dark-red plastic letters set against a grubby gold background, and as I drew closer, I saw the door had a hole in it at head height, as if somebody had punched it or hit it hard with something.

Before entering, I glanced back down the street. One of the prostitutes eyed a group of men who'd spilled from the pub. The other opened her coat to flash her red-and-black underwear and she giggled as she said to me, 'You can fuck me if you want?'

Desperate to get off the street, I pushed through the unlocked door into the stifling heat of a small, empty lobby entrance with a single high stool behind a tall desk and a cash register. The lobby led to a full-width staircase with purple carpet and shiny gold handrails, and I followed it up to a landing with glitzy, gold light fittings mounted on the walls.

I went past the rows of toilets and a cloakroom, and through a set of double doors where I found myself in the dim light of a large but near-empty casino. The vast expanse of the space took me by surprise given the tiny shops at street level, and I headed towards the long bar at the side of the room where most of the few people there had gathered.

A slow soulful song played softly in the background as I

walked between the roulette wheels and the green felt tables marked with colourful boxes.

Frilly lampshades suspended on cords from the ceiling hovered above the centre of each table, but most lights had been switched off and the only lights switched on were those at the far end of the casino where a handful of customers were playing.

A man in a white dinner jacket and bow tie caught my attention. He perched on a stool at the bar surrounded by three gruff men in baggy jumpers and dirty jeans, but before I got to them, an elegant middle-aged woman with make-up and big curly brown hair intercepted me.

She wore a sparkling silver dress and her big shoulder pads bulged as she leant down to me.

'Are you looking for someone?' she said in a thick cockney accent that didn't seem to suit her appearance.

'Roxy, tell the kid to fuck off,' the man in the white jacket shouted from the bar. 'We've got a license to keep hold of.'

'Leave him alone, he's only a boy,' Roxy replied, before she asked me, 'What do you want then? Are you lost?'

'I'm looking for Billy Apples. My Aunty Florence sent me.'

Roxy straightened and said, 'He wants to speak to you, Billy. He says his Aunty Florence sent him.'

The four men sat silently for a moment, before the man in the white jacket climbed off his stool.

'This should be fucking good,' he said. 'I only know one Florence, and she owes me money.'

'Is he a Brennan?' I heard one of the men at the bar say, as Roxy went to speak to them and Billy Apples came towards me.

I nervously clutched at the bag hanging around my waist and I blurted out without thinking. 'Brennan is my nan's old name, but I'm a Callaghan.'

'I can see that,' Billy Apples said in his flat, gravelly voice. 'I can see that a mile off, and that must make you Regan's boy.'

'Yes, I'm Jamie.'

'That's right, Jamie. You know, I thought I'd lost my money when I heard about your aunt.'

He had neat black hair and a square jaw, but his nose had been flattened and twisted out of its natural shape, and I wondered how he had managed to get a suntan when summer had long gone.

'Why are you here, kid?' he asked brusquely.

'Aunty Flo told me to give you these,' I said, and I removed the bank bonds from my bag and held them out. 'She said you'd give me the money for them.'

Billy's eyes widened as he took them from me. 'Where the fuck did you get these from?'

I went to say it's a long story, but he shut me down before I spoke.

'I don't want to know,' he said, as he flicked through the wad and assessed how much was there.

'Where have you come from?'

'Thatcham.'

'Where the fuck's that?'

'Berkshire.'

'Fuck me, kid. You're a long way from home. There's nothing stopping me from taking these from you, is there? The Brennans and the Callaghans, they've got no clout anymore. I could take these from you, and kick you out and there's nothing you could do about it, so why should I give you any money?'

'I need the money to help a friend,' I said.

'I need the money to help a friend,' he repeated, and he smirked. 'Everybody needs some money to help a friend, but why should I give it to you?'

'Her name is Freya,' I said, 'and it will help her.'

'Is it now?' Billy Apples said, and he laughed as he looked me up and down.

'Roxy!' he shouted over to the bar, and when she came over, he whispered in her ear and sent her away.

'I'll tell you what I'll do, kid,' Billy said. 'I'll give you half what these things are worth; half and no questions asked. You won't get better than that anywhere. I'm also going to take out what your Aunty Florence owes me, that's only fair, but all in all, you're getting a fucking good deal. Do you know why?'

'No,' I said.

'OK, kid,' he replied. 'I'll tell you why. One, I'm a fucking nice guy, and two, I liked your dad. We were pretty good mates when we were youngsters. We played football together, and went drinking, and he covered for me plenty of times when I got into a few scrapes. We even planned to go over to the States to see his Uncle Sid in Boston at one point, although we didn't quite manage to pull that off in the end.'

Billy stood there and nodded to himself as he enjoyed the nostalgia of his memories.

'But there was one thing that Regan taught me,' Billy added, 'and I've never forgotten it. Never run away from danger. If you're ever in danger, kid, always run towards it and meet it head on, never run away. If you run away, it will keep coming after you, and it will get you in the end.'

Roxy returned from a back room and handed Billy two large bundles of bank notes wrapped in elastic bands.

'I've just been telling the kid what a nice guy I am, Roxy,' Billy said.

'He doesn't look stupid enough to believe that,' Roxy replied.

'Come on, Billy,' one of the men called out from the bar. 'We've got business to sort out.'

'It was bloody sad what happened to Regan,' Billy said. 'If you were Conor's boy, I would have sent you packing with fuck all, but as you're Regan's kid, you get to walk out with this.'

He gave me the money and I put it in my bag.

'You be careful with all that money,' Roxy said, and she watched me intently. 'It might bring you an awful lot of heartache if you're not careful.'

I took a step back to leave as the men at the bar called over to Billy impatiently, and he returned to speak with them.

'Come with me,' Roxy said. 'I'll see you out.'

I followed her as she teetered on her high heels and asked me where I was going. After we had filed down the stairs into the lobby, she opened the front door for me.

I went out and the two prostitutes turned to face me.

'Hey, you lot!' Roxy shouted at them. 'You leave the kid alone, alright? He's with us.

'Now get going,' Roxy said to me. 'Go on, kid, scram. You've got a journey ahead of you.'

The women stepped aside, and a cold wind chased me down Brewer Street.

16

'She's a fucking bitch,' Aunty Flo said, leaning forward off her pillow to face down the ward.

A slim nurse with short curly brown hair and a clipboard under her arm disappeared into an office. As she crashed through the door, she appeared to glare back in Aunty Flo's direction.

'All the other nurses are lovely,' Aunty Flo added, 'but she's a right fucking cow.'

'Will you watch your language,' Nan hissed, 'there are sick people in here.'

'And you didn't ask for permission,' I chimed in.

'You don't need to talk to me about sick people.' Aunty Flo flicked her thumb at the withered old man in the bed behind me. He had a small, round, bald head and a pained expression on his face even as he slept. 'Nobody can get any bloody sleep with him groaning all night. As soon as the lights are turned down, he starts moaning and groaning non-stop all bloody night. No matter what they do, they can't shut him up.'

'Go easy on him,' Nan said, craning her neck past me to see. 'It doesn't look like he's got much longer.'

'Well, I wish he'd bloody well hurry up.'

'We brought you the things you wanted, Aunty Flo,' I interrupted before she had a chance to say anything more. I gave her a carrier bag full of cigarettes and the latest *Racing Post*.

'Well done, Jamie,' she said, peering inside. 'Right, let's go and get some fresh air. Jamie, fetch me one of those wheelchairs. They keep some spares on the other side of the nurses' station.'

I went to get the wheelchair and passed a nurse scribbling notes at the desk. She had wavy red hair tied up under her nurse's cap.

'Excuse me,' she said, as I wheeled the chair past. 'Can I ask where you're taking that?'

'It's for my aunty,' I said, pointing, 'that lady there, four beds down. Her name's—'

'Oh, don't worry.' She beamed. 'I know very well who your aunty is. You must be Jamie. She's told me all about you and it's a pleasure to finally meet you. I'm Julia.'

The smattering of freckles sprinkled across her porcelain skin reminded me of Freya. She slid the paperwork into a tray and when she stood up, a shaft of sunlight thrown from the window glistened in her pale-blue eyes.

'Let's go and have a little chat with your Aunty Florence, shall we?' The nurse placed a slender hand on my back and gracefully guided me across the ward. For a passing moment, her subtle fragrance masked the smell of hospital chemicals and disinfectant.

'Ah, Julia!' Aunty Flo cried out when she saw us coming. 'How is my favourite nurse today?'

'I'm very well, thank you, Florence, and I hope you are too? Did you get any sleep last night?'

'Not a bloody wink. There must be some other ward we can dump this bloke in.'

I sat down and Nurse Julia eased past my chair. She referred to the upside-down watch attached to her uniform as she felt for Aunty Flo's pulse.

'Sorry, we're stuck with him, I'm afraid,' Julia said, and she motioned down the ward to the office. 'And I trust nothing unpleasant has happened today?'

'If you are asking me if Nurse MacDonald has been unpleasant today,' Aunty Flo said, 'then the answer is no. Not yet anyway.'

'She was just doing her job.'

'She was extremely rude. It was completely unnecessary.'

'You were a little rude yourself. Things got very silly, very quickly. It would be nice if you would consider apologising.'

'I will not,' Aunty Flo said abruptly. 'I will not apologise. She should apologise to me. All I wanted was a bit of fresh air. I can't believe the way she spoke to me. It was completely uncalled for. I'm not having that.'

Julia thrust a thermometer into Aunty Flo's mouth, ostensibly to take her temperature.

'Nurse MacDonald was simply pointing out that if you want some fresh air, we can open your window, or you can sit in the very pleasant garden area outside the nurses' area. We both know the fresh air in the loading bay isn't very good for you.'

'I like the loading bay.'

'You should stay out of the loading bay. You've had a

serious stroke, and we want to get you better, but we can't do that if you don't look after yourself.'

'It wasn't serious,' Aunty Flo said, with a defiant wave of her good arm. 'There's nothing wrong with me. I'm absolutely fine. Just ask Dr Bryant, he'll tell you.'

In the fortnight since her stroke, I'd lost count of the times Aunty Flo had said there was nothing wrong with her, and I wondered whether she did truly believe it herself.

The distortions to her face had completely receded, but only limited use had returned to her left arm, and fatigue would set in quickly during our daily visits. 'I need to study the form,' she would say, picking up the *Racing Post* and sending us away when she grew tired.

But it was the change in her speech I found most disturbing. She spoke in the same manner and said all the same things she had always said, but there was now a split-second delay before each riposte which had never been there before.

Julia picked up the clipboard hanging at the bottom of the bed. 'Doctor Bryant is very fond of you,' she said, 'but that doesn't mean you're not seriously ill.'

'My progress has been exceptional,' Aunty Flo said.

'And he's been going to the betting shop for you as well, hasn't he?' Julia didn't look up from the clipboard when she asked.

'He goes to the betting shop of his own accord,' Aunty Flo replied a little defensively, 'and he is kind enough to place a modest bet for me while he's there.'

'He thinks you're a genius. We all went out after work on Friday, and he bought all the drinks with his winnings. He wouldn't stop talking about it. You have a gift at picking winners, apparently.'

'I have been known to have a little success from time to time.'

'We were all quite surprised to hear he's been gambling so much,' Julia said, and she looked up from her notes. 'We all met his wife at the Christmas party last year and we can't imagine she'd be too pleased to hear he's been in the bookmaker's every day, even if he has won some money.'

'There's no pleasing some people, is there?' Aunty Flo said, desperately trying to avoid eye contact with Nan.

Nurse MacDonald emerged from the office to speak with a doctor.

'Don't say a word,' Nan rapped as Aunty Flo sat forward.

'You should be kinder to her, Florence,' Julia said. 'Kate is a good friend of mine and she is an excellent nurse. She's only doing what she thinks is best for you.'

'She should be kinder to me,' Aunty Flo said. She took her time and then delivered the ace up her sleeve. 'It's not my fault if that surgeon she's been carrying on with won't leave his wife. She shouldn't take it out on the patients if she's not happy in her private life.'

Julia leant forward on the bed and hissed, 'How on earth do you know about that?'

Aunty Flo held her tongue and enjoyed the moment.

'Nobody knows about that,' Julia whispered. 'Nobody apart from me. How could you possibly know?'

'Well,' Aunty Flo said, 'I'm not blind, and I'm not stupid. I keep my eyes open, and I can see what's going on, and it's as plain as day what's going on there.'

It was Nurse Julia's turn to remain quiet. She pushed herself up off the bed and stood dumbstruck.

'Despite what Dr Bryant says,' Aunty Flo continued.

'I'm no genius. Far from it, but I know people and I know what makes them tick. And the minute I saw your friend Kate with that surgeon, I knew what was going on, and I knew she was besotted with him, and he would string her along until he got bored. And it won't be long now. He'll be moving on soon enough and if you look behind you, you'll see exactly where he'll be heading to next.'

Julia glanced over her shoulder to see a nurse across the aisle attending an elderly man with a jaundiced complexion. 'What? Elaine? Surely not?'

'You mark my words,' Aunty Flo said with a quiet authority. 'She's not enough to take him away from his wife, but he's already set his sights, and she won't be a difficult conquest. Just give it time. Poor Kate will soon know what betrayal is and all the pain that comes with it.'

Aunty Flo emphasised the word betrayal, and when she did so, Nan looked up sharply. The two sisters held each other's gaze for what seemed like a long time, and they appeared to speak to one another without talking.

'For once,' Nan said, 'I think you might be right about something, Gillian.'

Aunty Flo raised her eyebrows. 'Oh yeah, what's that?'

'There is nothing wrong with you.'

'You need to tell her to break it off with him,' Aunty Flo told Julia. 'You do that, and I'll apologise when I see her next.'

The pretty nurse returned the clipboard to the end of Aunty Flo's bed. 'Alright, you've got a deal,' Julia said. 'I'll do it. But you need to stop your trips to the loading bay.'

'That's going a bit too far, dear, but if you move this guy so he doesn't keep me up tonight, I might just consider cutting down a bit.'

Julia moved on to the old man in the bed next door. She turned and shook her head. 'Moving him won't be necessary,' she said sadly, and she pulled the curtain around his bed.

Aunty Flo's good right hand punched the air in delight. 'Yes,' she cried out. 'Jamie, go and get me that wheelchair.'

A reversing lorry beeped into one of the bays of the loading dock as we arrived. Smoke spewed from its exhaust.

Nurse Julia had a point. Between the fumes from the lorries and the odour from the bank of industrial-size bins lined up against the wall, the air was anything but fresh.

'Here we are,' Aunty Flo said cheerfully.

Two kitchen staff dressed in white stood away to our right, under a canopy covering a forklift truck, and Aunty Flo shared a knowing nod with them as they sucked at their cigarettes.

Nan lit two cigarettes and handed one to Aunty Flo, who leaned back and wriggled into her wheelchair to get comfortable.

Another patient, a young man wearing a red-and-green striped dressing gown, limped out on crutches to join us. He waved and said, 'Afternoon, Florence,' as he took out his packet of cigarettes. They shared a joke about his gammy leg and complained about the food before he returned to his ward.

When he'd gone, Nan said to Aunty Flo, 'You need to be careful with that doctor. He's got no idea what he's mixed up in, and he's not being discreet by the sound of things. The last thing you need right now is the police knocking on his front door.'

'Don't worry,' Aunty Flo said. 'I'm not stupid. I've fed him a couple of losers as well.'

'Well, you need to give him some more or, better still, cut him out of it completely.'

I aimed the questions at both of them. 'Why would the police knock on his door? Why would the police be interested in a few bets?'

'Now look what you've done,' Aunty Flo said to Nan.

'It's nothing, love,' Nan said. She cast a scowl down at her sister, but Aunty Flo had been distracted.

'Here he is,' Aunty Flo announced, and I heard Neil's voice behind me.

'Larry's here,' he said. 'Larry's in the hospital.'

'The whole gang's here,' Aunty Flo said. She finished her second cigarette and let it fall to the floor, twisting her foot into it. 'Let's go and see him. Come on, Jamie. Did Nurse Julia tell you we were down here, Neil?'

'What's wrong, love?' Nan asked.

Neil restlessly kneaded his forehead with the tips of his fingers.

'What is it, Neil?' Nan pressed, more urgently this time.

'It's Larry, he's been mugged,' Neil said. 'He's in Battle block. He was walking back through the alleyway when they jumped him. He's in a bad way. I was driving home down Paynesdown Road when I saw the ambulance and I saw him on the stretcher. They treated him there for a while and then I followed the ambulance here. They've taken him to Battle block.'

'Right, let's go,' Nan said, setting off for the door.

I wheeled Aunty Flo into the lift lobby. Nan and Neil were deep in conversation as they waited for the lift. When they'd finished speaking, Nan said to me, 'Take your aunt back to the ward, it's best I go alone.'

The lift came. Nan and Neil got in and they went up and left us.

'Who would mug an old man like Larry?' I asked Aunty Flo.

She didn't respond, and she stared blankly at a noticeboard on the wall.

'Take me back outside, Jamie,' she said.

'Why? Do you want some more fresh air?'

'No, dear,' she replied. 'I need a fag.'

17

It wasn't until the Christmas decorations had been put up that both Aunty Flo and Larry were able to leave hospital.

Larry could have been released earlier, but for reasons that weren't altogether clear to me, he'd been reluctant to do so.

'They want to discharge Larry,' I'd overheard Nan say to Uncle Tom on the phone. 'They want to get the bed back, but he keeps stalling for time, complaining about stomach cramps and dizzy spells and whatnot so he can stay longer.'

And it wasn't until Aunty Flo received notice she could come home that Larry finally agreed to leave.

Nan broke the news over breakfast. After spending the weekends and every evening after school at the hospital, it came as a relief that things would soon return to normal.

After finishing my cereal, I pulled on my coat, collected my bag, and headed out for school. At the garages opposite Larry's house, the memory of my first visit to see him in hospital came back to me.

Nan had tried to warn me. On our way there she repeated several times, 'The bastards have beaten him up pretty bad,' but on reflection, there was nothing she could have said to properly prepare me.

He lay there motionless, his head turned to one side, with his mouth wide open as he slept. A bright white padded bandage covered a cut above his left eye and the bruises down the side of his unshaven face and neck had turned into a burnt yellowy-brown colour.

I had expected to find him on a ward, but he had a room to himself where he'd been hooked up to a monitor with a series of wires and a transparent tube taped to the underside of his nose.

The pulsing display and repetitive bleeps on the monitor made me nervous. I thought, at any moment, it would flatline, like it always seems to do on the TV, and a gang of panicked doctors and nurses would suddenly burst through the door and try, in vain, to save him.

Larry slept for a long while and when he did come around, he said slowly, 'Hello, Jamie, thank you for coming to see me.'

I handed over the newspaper and sweets we'd brought him and answered his questions about school and Freya as cheerfully as I could.

A stout nurse came in with his dinner on a trolley. I'd heard her booming laugh in the corridor, where she'd been joking with the other patients, but her demeanour changed when she entered. 'Come on, Larry,' she said gravely, 'you must try to eat something.'

Larry reluctantly picked up his fork for a couple of small mouthfuls while the nurse remained, but as soon as she'd left the room, he did little more than push the food around the plate. It was only at Nan's insistence that he ate anything more.

After his meal, Larry wanted to sleep, so we said our goodbyes and left him to go over to Caversham Ward to see Aunty Flo.

'I saw Larry today,' she said when we arrived. 'I got one of the trainee nurses to wheel me over there.'

'How was he?' Nan asked.

'Fine,' Aunty Flo replied before changing the subject. It was all too evident they didn't want to talk about him in front of me.

On the bus home later that night, I asked Nan, 'Will the police find the people that hurt Larry?'

'No, love.'

'But they must have some chance of catching them? Somebody must have seen something?'

She didn't look at me; her eyes remained fixed on the dark streets outside and a little anger crept into her voice. 'They won't find them, Jamie. They just won't. It's not always like the TV, you know. Sometimes there is no happy ending, sometimes there is no justice. It's just something you've got to get used to.'

Aunty Flo and Larry came home together on the Friday evening. Neil picked them up in his van and Nan laid on a buffet so we could have a little welcome-home party. I was put in charge of drinks.

'I invited Julia and Kate tonight, Bet, but they couldn't make it,' Aunty Flo said as she snatched a ham sandwich from a platter on the dining room table.

'Who are they?' Neil asked.

'Nurses at the hospital,' Aunty Flo said. 'You know

Kate. Kate MacDonald, we talked about her. She's the one you said was nice.'

Neil looked up from his plate of food. 'Did I?'

'Yes, yes, you must remember,' Aunty Flo insisted. 'I said, "Do you think she's nice?" and you said you did and we agreed to invite her over one night. Remember?'

'No?' Neil shrugged.

'Well, you did,' Aunty Flo said. 'I can't believe you don't remember.'

Nan shouted through the archway, 'Jamie, will you get me one of those as well, love?'

I reached for another glass and filled it from the cask of Neil's home brew.

I gave Nan and Aunty Flo their drinks and when I handed Larry his, I noticed his hand trembling terribly. I retreated to the corner and, from across the room, I studied Larry carefully. He stood quietly, leaning on the back of a dining room chair. He'd lost so much weight his jumper and the shirt underneath appeared to hang off him.

The bruising had healed but his face had become gaunt, with cheekbones cutting at angles below eyes now vacant and sunken and drooping at the sides. He remained unshaven, as he had been each time I'd seen him in hospital, with his aging skin interspersed with patches of scruffy grey stubble.

'Oh, that's awful,' Aunty Flo said, as she tasted Neil's beer.

Nan passed through to the kitchen to collect a tray of sausage rolls and she pulled me to one side. 'Go and put some music on, love,' she said, 'and I'm just letting you know, you might have to sleep on the settee tonight. I'm not sure Larry wants to go home alone, so he might need your bed.'

I went to the lounge and put a record on. The stylus crackled and the music began. Over the sound of Christmas pop music, I heard raised voices and the dogs yapping in the kitchen.

'Jamie!' Nan shouted. 'Freya's here.'

I thought I'd misheard, but at the doorway to the kitchen, I found Freya standing inside our back door, staring down the length of the room at me.

'Come on in, love,' Nan said, helping Freya remove her coat. 'It's chilly out there, isn't it?'

'Yes, but it's nice and warm in here,' Freya said. 'I hope you don't mind me coming over. I saw Larry and Aunty Flo get out of Neil's van and I wanted to come and say welcome home.'

'No, of course we don't mind,' Nan said, hanging up Freya's coat. 'It's lovely to see you. I guess your dad's at Sergeant Meadows' leaving party tonight? He's only got a few weeks left now, hasn't he?'

'Yes, that's right,' Freya said, and she slipped off her shoes and skipped over to Larry.

She embraced him with eyes closed and she buried her head deep into his chest.

Larry patted and stroked her back. He whispered something in her ear, and she tightened her grip when he said it.

The hug lingered and when Freya finally released Larry, Aunty Flo said, 'Come on over here, dear, it must be my turn now.'

'Are you hungry, Freya?' Nan asked. 'Can I get you something to eat?'

'No thanks, I'm fine. I've just had my dinner.'

'What about something to drink? We've got some lemonade.'

'That would be nice, thank you.'

'Jamie, get Freya some lemonade, will you please, love?'

'Oh, and, Jamie,' Aunty Flo said, holding out her empty glass, 'get me a refill while you're out there.'

I made the drinks in the kitchen and returned to find Nan and Aunty Flo fussing over Freya.

'So, what do you think of all these new Christmas songs?' Aunty Flo asked her. 'Jamie and Neil keep putting them on, but we like the old classics, don't we, Bet?'

'I like them,' Freya said. 'I love the one that's playing now. It's one of my favourites.'

'Oh no, Freya, love,' Nan said, 'the old songs are the best. These new pop songs can't compete with the golden oldies.'

'You two both love these songs,' I said to Nan and Aunty Flo, and Neil nodded in agreement. 'You couldn't get enough of them at Uncle Pat's party last year,' I went on. 'He put on an old slow one and you both told him to change it so you could carry on dancing.'

'No, that can't be right,' Aunty Flo said, and she screwed up her face and flicked her wrist to wave the suggestion away.

'You definitely did,' I said, 'and you both ganged up on Pat until he changed it.'

'Really?' Nan said. 'I don't remember that.'

'They definitely did,' I said to Freya, and she hinted at a laugh.

'Alright then,' Nan said. 'We'll leave these songs on for now and we'll get some of the oldies on later.'

Nan moved away to get some food and Freya joined me in the corner of the room. 'You looked surprised to see me.'

'I was surprised. I had no idea you were coming. What if your dad finds out?'

'It's OK, he won't. He said he'd be out until late tonight.'

'That's good. I'm glad you came, but I don't want you to get into trouble.'

We observed as Aunty Flo held court with Larry and Neil flanked on either side and Nan's side profile made up the fourth side of a square.

Nan reached over to pick up her glass from the table. She grinned at us before taking a swig of her drink and returning to the group to berate Aunty Flo.

After the elation of her arrival, Freya's mood quickly lapsed into melancholy. Her eyes, now bloodshot and threatening tears, fixed on Larry.

'Larry will be OK,' I said reassuringly, but she appeared not to hear. She remained silent and distant, and I wanted badly to know what she was thinking.

I tried to open up conversations about teachers and pupils at school, but she did little more than respond each time with a tame smile.

My mind raced. I had planned to do things differently. I had planned to talk to Freya alone in a quiet corner of the school, but in my despair at her sadness, I decided to tell her there and then.

A Christmas song finished, and the jingle of sleigh bells introduced the next.

'Listen,' I said. 'I've got something to tell you. It's important. Are you listening?'

'Yes,' she said. 'What is it?'

'Nobody knows, nobody, not even Nan, but I've got some money for you. I've got enough so you can run away. You can get away from your dad. You can go to your auntie's in Suffolk. I can tell you how to get there; I've worked it all out, which trains you need to get and what times they go, and I've got enough money for you, for the train and lots more you can give to your aunty and uncle so they can buy you everything you need when you start to live there.'

'No, Jamie,' she replied. 'No, I can't run away. Not now, it's not important, not at the moment.'

Aunty Flo bellowed a punchline, and we turned to see the others dissolve into laughter.

'You've got to tell your nan to stop,' Freya said, and she grabbed my arm to emphasise her point. 'She's got to stop and if she doesn't, things will get even worse. You've got to make her. Make her stop and get her to tell my dad she's stopped.'

'What?' I asked. 'What do you mean "stop"? Stop what?'

'I don't know what it is exactly but whatever she's doing she's got to stop it, because if she doesn't my dad will do something awful. I've heard him talk with his friends. Please, Jamie, please, you've got to tell her.'

Stan barked and Nan told him to be quiet. She glanced over at Freya and I and the smile fell from her face. She'd sensed we were talking about something serious.

'I don't understand,' I said. 'She's not doing anything. How can she stop if she's not doing anything?'

'There are things going on that we don't know about,' Freya said, and when she said it, I got the impression she knew more than she was letting on.

'Alright, let's tell Nan now. We can tell her together. Come on, let's do it now.'

'No, I don't want to,' Freya said. 'Please, Jamie. Please don't make me.'

'OK,' I replied. 'OK, I'll tell her to stop. When you've gone, I'll tell her. Whatever it is she's doing, I'll tell her to stop it.'

The square broke apart. Larry and Neil picked at the buffet, and Nan filed through to the kitchen.

Aunty Flo came over to us. 'What are you two talking about, then?'

'Nothing,' I said more abruptly than intended.

Aunty Flo ignored my tone and asked, 'Is it the first time you've been here, Freya? I guess it's the same as your house, but everything's back to front?'

Freya managed a smile. 'Yes, everything is the wrong way around.'

She surveyed the dining room and the arch through to the kitchen. 'We have a door there,' she said, 'we don't have an archway. And we've got a bathroom downstairs, over there.' She pointed to the corner of the dining room. 'A disabled person lived there before us and the Council never removed it.'

'And I bet your house isn't as hot as this one,' Aunty Flo said. 'Jamie and his nan turn the thermostat all the way up and it's always bloody roasting, way too hot for me. I'm used to my little caravan in Hayling Island.'

The back door swung violently open and clattered a cupboard.

Vic Dyson filled the doorway.

He yanked at the tie around his neck to pull it loose

and, as he did so, the collar of his untucked grey flannel shirt twisted out of shape.

Freya clutched at my arm.

'Where is she?' Vic shouted, his voice harsh and guttural.

He saw his daughter through the archway, and he stepped inside across the threshold. He pointed and bellowed, 'You, get home now!'

Stan had been barking at the door before it had been thrown open, and although I didn't see it, I suspected the door had hit him. Whether it did or not, Stan now roused himself and charged forward, barking furiously. Vic took a stride and kicked out. His foot connected with the side of Stan's head, and it sent him sprawling across the kitchen tiles.

Neil, who stood in the archway closest to Vic, reacted first. 'Hey,' he cried out, leaping forward to gather up Stan.

Vic intercepted and he swung a fist at Neil. The punch didn't connect properly, instead cuffing the back of Neil's head where he had ducked down to pick up Stan, but there was enough contact to throw Neil off balance and he fell to the floor.

Before Neil could scramble to his feet, Vic struck him again, this time full in the face, and I heard a sickening sound above the Christmas bells chiming from the stereo. Blood squirted from Neil's nose and his head snapped back onto the hard surface of the kitchen floor.

It was clear Neil couldn't fight back after the first blow, but Vic punched him again and again, twice more while Neil lay there, unable to defend himself.

As this happened, everyone seemed to cry out at the same time and clamour forward to defend Neil.

In amongst the screaming, I heard Freya plead, 'Stop, please stop.' I slipped and skidded to the floor while she flung herself into her father's torso, to stifle any further punches. 'I'm sorry,' she cried. 'I'm sorry, please.'

Nan came past me. Vic twisted around and I thought he would hit her too. I grabbed Nan's cardigan to hold her back and I felt the wool stretch in my fingertips.

'Get out. Get out of here!' Nan shrieked in a shrill and piercing scream.

'I've warned you!' Vic shouted back. Spit and the stench of alcohol spilled from his mouth.

'Please stop, please stop,' Freya continued to cry. She clung to her father's body to subdue him, but he had worked his right arm free.

He shaped to lash out at Nan. I got to my feet, and I threw myself between them. Vic grabbed my shoulder and shoved me into the cupboards. 'I've fucking warned you!' he shouted at Nan.

Aunty Flo and I grabbed hold of Nan and Freya clasped herself around Vic. The two parties stood off from one another in the middle of the kitchen.

Neil remained on the floor with his face and shirt covered in blood, but he'd recovered enough to take hold of Stan, who pulled against his grip to snarl aggressively at Vic.

'Get out!' Nan screamed again, pointing to the door. 'Get out of my house.'

Vic breathed heavily and glared down at Nan before Freya managed to half turn him to the door.

'That's it, no more fucking chances!' Vic roared. He dragged Freya outside and they were gone.

We later found out, through a conversation Aunty Flo had with a couple of young guys in The Cricket's pub, that Vic had left the retirement party early after he'd had an argument with a detective constable. Scuffles had broken out when the pair squared up to each other in the football-club car park, before some fellow party guests had diffused the situation and sent Vic on his way.

I went over to the window and watched as Vic and Freya disappeared inside their dark and empty house.

'We've got to help her,' I said to Nan, but her eyes closed, and she subtly shook her head.

Aunty Flo dropped to her knees and crouched over Neil. She wiped away the blood from his nose and the side of his mouth with a tissue.

'I'm alright,' Neil said, and he sat up and stroked Stan, who'd remained at his side.

Through the archway, I saw Larry still standing in the dining room, leaning on the back of a dining room chair with a trembling hand covering his mouth.

Nan went slowly over to the back door and closed it. We waited for her to speak.

'Jamie,' she said finally, in a belligerent but calm voice, 'go and turn that music off.'

18

I set off early for school on Monday morning.

An unspoken rule had developed between Freya and I where, out of a fear of being seen by her dad, we would avoid any form of contact on our journeys to and from school.

Determined to break that rule, I waited for Freya at the back of the garages, and I called her over when she eventually trudged past on the frosty pavement.

'We can't see each other anymore,' she rapped. The knitted bobble hat she wore had pushed her fringe down over the top of her eyes, so she tilted her head back when she spoke to me.

'I know, I'm sorry, but please just listen for a few minutes.'

'Make it quick. I've got something to tell you as well, but that's it, we can't let anything else happen.'

'Take this,' I said, taking an envelope from my inside coat pocket and placing it in her palm. 'This is the money I told you about. Take it and run away, go and live with your aunt.'

Freya looked inside the envelope at the stack of banknotes neatly bundled together. 'Jamie,' she said, 'where did you get this from?'

'Aunty Flo gave it to me, for something special or an emergency. Take it. I want you to have it. I don't need it.'

'I can't take it. It's too much.'

'No, you've got to take it. This is your chance.'

'No, I don't—'

I cut in. Speaking quickly, I said, 'You can't stay here with him anymore. Not now; you've got to leave. You'll be happy with your aunty and uncle, but you'll never be happy here with him.'

She didn't argue, and I maintained momentum by pointing out the piece of paper and the two folded maps in the envelope.

'There are instructions to get you to your aunt's house. I've written everything down for you and I've included maps of the train lines and the underground. Catch the London train to Paddington and then take the underground to Liverpool Street. It's easy, you can do it, just follow the instructions. The train timetables are all there for you. When you get to Liverpool Street, catch another train to Ipswich. From Ipswich you can take a taxi or phone your aunt to collect you. There's enough money for the trains and the taxi and there will be plenty left over for any new things you need when you get there. Everything you need to get away is here.'

'Jamie, it's too much. I can't take it from you.'

'You've got to take it. This is our chance. Go before things get worse.'

'But I can't pay you back.'

'You don't need to,' I said, and then I started to say, 'when we're older...' but I trailed off mid-sentence.

Over the weekend I'd practised everything I'd said up until this point, but I'd now strayed into unrehearsed territory.

'It doesn't matter,' I said tamely, before reverting to script. 'Go on Friday after school, so you've got the weekend to go through things with your aunt and uncle. They can phone the school on Monday.'

'I don't know, Jamie,' Freya said, and she looked over her shoulder nervously as a group of older kids walked noisily past. 'Maybe it's better I stay. I can try to find out more if I stay. He's planning something, I know he is. I don't know what exactly, but I think your nan is in danger. Something's happening on the 19th. I overheard him on the phone to one of his friends. He mentioned her name and then he went on to say everything must be done by the 19th. I'm not sure, I might be wrong, but if I am right, and it's the 19th of this month, that's less than two weeks away.'

'What else did he say?' I asked and, as I did so, I saw Tommy Rayner gawping at us from the road.

'What are you two doing?' he called out with a stupid smirk etched on his face.

I said, 'I'll see you at break.' I waved him on, but instead of moving on, he slowed to a standstill.

'Come on, tell me,' Tommy said. 'What's going on with you two?'

'Not now, Tommy,' I said seriously. 'Just go and I'll see you later.'

He muttered something and reluctantly pulled away.

I turned back to Freya. 'Did you hear anything else? Anything? Anything else about the 19th?'

'I don't know,' Freya said, raising a hand to her mouth. 'Maybe I'm wrong. Maybe it's something else. Maybe it's nothing to do with your nan. I don't know, I'm just worried. If I stay, I can find out more.'

'No, you've got to go,' I said. 'Go while you can. Don't worry, I'll sort things out this end with Nan. I know what to do. You must go on Friday.'

'What are you going to do?'

'It doesn't matter. Just go and let me know you've got there safely. I've written our phone number on the piece of paper in there.'

'Alright, I'll try,' she said. 'How's Neil? Please tell him I'm so sorry I came over. I wish I hadn't.'

'He's fine. Aunty Flo didn't want him to, but he's gone to work today. She made him some soup over the weekend. I've never seen her cook anything before. It was disgusting but he's been eating it. Please don't feel bad. It's not your fault. None of us blame you.'

I thought she would cry, but she held off the tears. 'I've made such a mess of everything,' she said.

'No, it's not your fault,' I replied. Gaining strength from her weakness, I said confidently, 'Get to your aunt's. You'll be safe there, and I'll make sure things work out here. Everything will be fine. I promise.'

Freya pushed the envelope deep into her satchel.

Her brown eyes lingered on mine, and she said, 'Thank you, Jamie. I won't forget this, but please, you must make sure nothing happens to your nan.'

Her lips warmed my cold cheek when she kissed me, and I watched her walk away.

I didn't move for some time, and not until a young

mother pushing a pram cast a suspicious glance in my direction when she noticed me loitering.

As I emerged from the side of the garages, I saw the spot across the street, outside Larry's house, where I gave Freya the clock. It felt like a long time ago. I wondered where the clock was now and, although I knew the chances were slim, I hoped Freya would take it with her when she left.

I walked to school and endured a long, tedious week.

When Friday afternoon did finally come, I returned home, dumped my bag down and made tea. Nan and Aunty Flo had gone out to do some shopping and Neil had yet to arrive home from work. With the house to myself, I went upstairs and leant on the windowsill of Nan's bedroom window to wait and watch for Freya to leave.

Dusk fell as I surveyed the street. Orange lamp posts spluttered into life, and multicoloured Christmas lights of red, blue, yellow, and green lit up windows in the rows of houses stretching away up Paynesdown Road.

Freya's house remained dark, as it always had been, with all curtains drawn to black out any signs of life.

A seed of doubt had crept into my thoughts earlier that day, and as I waited and time dragged slowly by, the idea that Freya would reverse her decision and elect to stay now began to flourish.

I made up my mind. At 5pm I would go across the road and try again to persuade her to leave. I thought over what I would say and I rehearsed the speech to convince her over and over, but at 4:52pm, Freya appeared.

She wore her bobble hat and heavy winter coat with a bulging rucksack strapped across her back. She'd given herself plenty of time to catch the 5:53pm train. Her dad wouldn't be home from work for at least another hour, so she locked the door and slid the key under an empty flowerpot.

When she closed the gate behind her, I hoped she would look up and see me, but she didn't. With her face set with determination, she started up Paynesdown Road for the station. I watched her walk away from me for the second time that week and as she disappeared out of view, something inside told me, quite correctly, as things transpired, that I would never see her again.

I whispered goodbye and my warm breath misted over a small patch of window. It remained for a fleeting moment, and then vanished as quickly as it had appeared.

With Freya gone, I turned my attention to the second phase of my plan. I had to get Nan safe.

Later that night, after we'd all settled down in front of the TV, I clumsily blurted out, 'Nan, you've got to tell Vic you'll stop.'

I'd been stewing all evening, and I'd been desperate to say it around the dining room table, but with Aunty Flo fussing over Neil all through dinner, the right moment didn't arrive.

Nan's knitting needles stopped clicking. 'What?'

'You've got to tell him.'

'Jamie, calm down,' Nan tried to interrupt but I talked over her.

'Whatever you're doing, whatever it is, I know you won't tell me, but I don't care. Just go and tell him, tell him you'll stop. Go and do it tonight. You've got to put an end to this.'

'Jamie, Jamie, slow down,' Nan said. 'Neil, be a love and turn the telly down.'

Neil fumbled for the TV control.

'If you don't tell him,' I said. 'I'll go and tell him myself. I'll tell him you'll stop.'

'You will not,' Nan said, raising her voice. I'd made her angry. She dropped the knitting into her lap, and she pointed at me. 'You listen to me. You will do no such thing. After what he did to Neil, do you really think we're going to back down?'

'We've got to,' I said, and my words strained. 'We've got no choice. He is going to do something terrible. Aunty Flo is still poorly and look what's happened to Larry and Neil. We can't let anything else happen.'

Aunty Flo stubbed out her cigarette. 'Don't you worry about me,' she said defiantly. 'I'm absolutely fine. It's Freya you should be worried about. We can't just give in to him and abandon her, can we?'

'Freya's safe,' I said. 'She's gone to her aunt and uncle's in Ipswich. She left earlier tonight on the 5:53pm train.'

'How do you know that?' Aunty Flo asked.

'I told her to go, and I helped her. I had to get her away from him.'

'She'll be back, Jamie,' Nan said. 'They won't keep her there against her father's wishes.'

'They will keep her,' I said. 'She'll tell them what he did and they'll keep her safe.'

'No, they won't,' Nan said. 'Sorry, Jamie, but it's not that easy. We tried that a long time ago. She'll be back here soon enough, just you wait and see. She'll be back and if we give in to him, we'll be no better off. I know you mean well, love, but it's better you stay out of it.'

'No, I won't stay out of it!' I shouted. 'I know I'm right.

You've got to listen to me. You've got to tell Vic you'll stop. Freya told me, she told me before she left that's he's planning something; he's going to hurt you, he's already planning it. You've got to tell him before the 19th.'

'He's planning what?' Aunty Flo asked.

'I don't know, but whatever it is, it's going to be bad.'

'What did Freya say, Jamie?' Nan asked.

'I just told you. He's planning something for 19th. You've got to tell him, so he'll stop. Why won't you listen to me?'

'How does Freya know?'

'She overheard him on the phone to one of his friends. Freya's scared. She's scared of what he'll do, and I promised her I'd keep you safe.'

'We're not backing down, Jamie,' Nan said emphatically. 'I'm sorry, but we are not backing down. You've just got to trust me. We'll all be fine and everything will work out in the end.'

'No. No, it won't,' I said. Her dismissive reply had annoyed me, and it was my turn to be angry. 'It won't be alright, why don't you understand?' I got to my feet. 'We've got to end all this. It's the only way.'

Nan shook her head, and I stormed across the room for the stairs.

'She'll be back, you know,' Nan said after me. 'Freya will be sent back from her aunt's, just you wait and see.'

I slammed the door and pounded up the stairs.

I lay on my bed, seething for hours. The thought that Nan would prove me wrong, and Freya would be sent home, angered me every bit as much as her refusal to end the feud. I don't know what time I fell asleep, but I was still fully dressed and on top of the bed covers when Stan's solitary bark woke me.

I heard our gate hinges squeal, the back door open and a low rumble of voices. Through bleary eyes, the red digital numbers on my alarm clock displayed 1:03am.

I crept downstairs. After years of practice, I carefully stepped on the silent treads that wouldn't creak. I perched on the bottom step and listened at the dining room door for the voices behind it.

I heard Nan say, 'Come on, let's get started,' and murmurings from Aunty Flo, Neil and Larry.

Chair legs scraped across the carpet and teacups chinked on saucers as the four of them gathered around the table.

Nan began to speak, and her manner made it sound like the beginning of a formal meeting.

I knelt in front of the door and pressed my ear up close against it so I could hear every word.

'Alright, it looks like a change of plan,' she said. 'We've no choice but to go for Plan B. We do it next Friday night. The time has come to kill that fucking bastard.'

19

I spent the weekend hiding in my bedroom and, for most of it, I stared aimlessly out the window. Neighbours scraped at frosted windscreens and icicles dripped from frozen gutters, and I replayed Nan's words over and over in my mind.

Could they really be planning to kill Vic? I found it impossible to believe. The more I thought about it, the more absurd it all seemed.

I began to question whether I had actually heard her correctly? Did she really say "kill?" or did she say something else and I'd misheard?

At one point I even considered it might be part of an elaborate joke they'd all decided to play on me, before I quickly dismissed that idea as even more ludicrous.

My mind tossed and turned, but I kept coming back to the same questions.

Why would Nan want to kill Vic? What could he have possibly done to bring us to this? And why now? Why not before?

I only had one clear thought in my head. I had to stop them both.

In need of a distraction, I flopped on the bed and thumbed through the pages of a beaten-up book from the school library. I had one last piece of history homework to complete.

I read about Stalin's treacherous deal with Hitler. I read about Roosevelt, and how the Americans refused to help, and when de Gaulle's France were knocked out of the war, Great Britain stood alone against the might of Nazi Germany and the Axis powers. Sitting alone in my bedroom, it felt as though my problems were every bit as bad as Churchill's when he sat in London with the Luftwaffes' bombs raining down, and he prepared to fight his evil neighbour across the English Channel. I worked through the exercises, but they couldn't hold my attention for long.

I cleared out some old clothes from the wardrobe that didn't fit anymore and stacked up my weekly football magazines in date order. I thought I'd found a magazine I hadn't been through, but after scanning through a couple of articles, I realised I'd already read it.

With nothing to do, the temptation to head downstairs almost got the better of me, but I stopped myself at the top of the stairs and instead sneaked into Nan's empty bedroom.

From behind the curtain, I saw Vic's car parked on the drive, still iced over from the night before.

Freya hadn't phoned to tell me she'd arrived safely, and I wondered whether Vic knew where she was. Looking down on his still and seemingly untroubled house, I suspected he did know.

It occurred to me that Freya might have left him a note, or she may have phoned him when she'd arrived. But if the latter was true, why hadn't she let me know when I'd specifically asked her to? Maybe it wasn't Freya that had told her father, maybe it was her aunt?

A van passed outside, cautiously turning at the crossroads before speeding away up Paynesdown Road. When it had gone, it left me alone and in silence.

At dinner time, when I had no choice but to go downstairs, I ate my food quietly and waited politely for a gesture of reconciliation from Nan. It never came.

Neil struggled to cope with the tension. He fidgeted around more than usual and, at times, tried to plug the awkward gaps in conversation.

'That program you like is on tonight, Jamie,' he said enthusiastically. 'It's a Christmas special. Will you come down and watch it with us?'

'No, I don't think so,' I replied. 'I'll be in my room.'

The phone rang.

'I'll get it,' Nan said, and she hastily set off for the hall.

'Hello? Oh, hello, Sita,' she said. 'Can I call you back? We're in the middle of dinner.'

I tried to hide my disappointment, but my attempt evidently failed.

'No news from Freya yet, then?' Aunty Flo asked, picking up the salt shaker. 'I hope she's alright. We were talking about it late last night. You shouldn't have sent her off like that by herself. If we had her aunt's number, we could phone to make sure she got there, but we don't.'

'I'm sure she's alright,' Nan said, as she returned. 'We would have heard from Vic by now if he didn't know she was safe. But you can't do anything on your own like this again, love. You've got to tell us these things.'

I felt a swell of anger boil up inside me and all the bitterness of last night's argument came rushing back.

Ignoring everything they'd said, I asked Nan, 'What did Sita want?'

There was something in her manner when she took the call that stirred my interest.

'I don't know,' Nan said calmly. 'I'll call her back later.'

'Why didn't you talk to her?'

'I'm having my dinner, Jamie.'

'She'd do anything for you, wouldn't she?' I asked. 'She often says how much she owes you.'

Nan lowered her knife and fork. 'Sita doesn't owe me anything. I've helped her out once or twice, but I certainly didn't do it to get something in return. I hope you don't think like that, Jamie. I'd be extremely disappointed if you did. We've brought you up to be better than that. Right, I think we'll have pudding in front of the TV. If you want some, Jamie, you can join us in there.'

I immediately regretted the conversation. It had been pointless and served no useful purpose. They didn't know I'd overheard their plans for Vic and I wanted to keep it that way, and whether Sita was part of those plans or not, it made absolutely no difference. Whatever Nan and Aunty Flo said about doing things on my own, I had to find a way to intervene and appease both Nan and Vic before something unthinkable happened.

But by the following Wednesday, I still had no clear idea of what to do, and there still hadn't been any news from Freya. I was too caught up in my thoughts to remember walking home from school, but when I let myself in the back door, I found Nan in the kitchen baking with flecks of cake batter splattered up her navy-blue-and-white pinstriped apron.

'Everything alright at school?' she asked.

'Fine thanks.'

'Your Aunty Florence has gone to Newbury races,' Nan said, as she tapped a whisk on the rim of a mixing bowl. 'Neil's going to pick her up on his way home.'

I emptied out my bag, placed my lunchbox on the table, and told her I'd be in the lounge watching TV.

The dogs came through from their kitchen basket to join me after I'd fallen into my spot on the sofa. Stan jumped up onto my lap and Ollie nestled in alongside my thigh, and I thoughtlessly flicked through the channels. I inspected Ollie's eye. Nan had taken him to the vet on Monday, but his treatment had yet to show any signs of improvement and, if anything, the eye appeared to be as bad as it had ever been. Although Nan hadn't let on, I suspected her visit had come with a warning from the vet that Ollie would likely lose his eye, and with his other eye showing the early signs of infection, I couldn't help but fear the worst.

A loud banging noise came from the kitchen, and Stan leapt from my lap.

When I heard Nan shout, 'Oi,' I realised the sound had come from her thumping at the window.

'Oi, get out of it!' she yelled again.

I made it to the kitchen in time to watch Nan throw open the back door and chase across the lawn in her slippers.

Beyond her, I saw a cat at the bottom of the garden. I recognised it as the ginger tomcat from down the end of

Bourne Road. It had scars on its face from the late-night screeching fights we would often hear. A blackbird, caught by the wing, dangled from the cat's mouth. A second blackbird hovered above, frantically chirping and flapping its wings.

Stan raced ahead of Nan and as he closed in, the bird fell from its mouth and the tomcat bolted over our rear fence onto next door's driveway.

While Stan yapped at the fence, the blackbird sat motionless on the damp grass with its beak open.

I ran onto the cold and soggy lawn in my socks. 'Come on, fly away,' I urged in the desperate hope the poor creature would be able to.

'Hold back, love,' Nan said, 'give it some space.'

The bird didn't move. It sat perfectly still without the slightest of movements. Its companion had settled in its nest up in the conifers, cheeping occasionally as it peered down at the scene.

'I've got an idea. Wait there,' I said to Nan. I went to the kitchen and returned with a saucer of water and a slice of bread. I set them down in front of the blackbird and backed away.

The blackbird in the conifers hesitated at first, but eventually swooped down and busily pecked at the bread, but its injured companion wouldn't stir.

We waited for some time, hoping for a recovery. I didn't want to ask, but I knew I couldn't escape the question forever. 'Nan, will it live?'

'No, love,' she said quietly. 'It's got a broken wing. I got out here too late to save it.'

She walked over and gathered up the wounded bird,

cupping both hands around its body, before taking it over to the conifers and stretching up to place it in its nest.

'I've never told you before, have I?' she said on her way back to me. It was more of a statement than a question. 'The cats always get them; they always kill our blackbirds. We never told you because we knew you'd be upset, but it happens every year. Me and your grandad would try our best to fight them off, but in the end, we never could save them.'

I looked up at the dying blackbird in the conifers. Its beak had closed, and it had started to move again as it settled in the nest. The other blackbird had returned to stand on the rim, and when it chirped at its damaged companion, it reminded me of Nan trying to get Grandad out of bed in the early afternoon, encouraging him to get up, to get dressed, to go on with life.

'At least the cats won't get it now,' Nan said. 'At least it'll die with some dignity. It's not much of a victory, but it is something.' She turned to face me. 'We did what we could, love. That's what we do. We fight our battles as best as we can and we hope it's good enough. I don't know about you, but I couldn't live with myself if I stood by and did nothing.'

I studied the creases on her face. They appeared to cut longer and deeper today. She looked old and tired and behind the thick-rimmed glasses, her blue eyes seemed to be full of sorrow.

I remembered the story Aunty Flo had told me on the way to Oxford, when, against all odds, Nan had fought back against the nuns. I thought of Grandad's letters and what he had to do to survive in the war as he fought his way across

Belgium, and I recalled how Nan and Larry had busted Grandad out of hospital when he was desperate to escape the cruel treatment of the doctors there.

And it made me think there must be other stories, other stories from their lives that I'd not yet been told, and maybe I never would be.

She stared back at me intently, searching deep inside as though she were reading my thoughts.

'Believe me,' she started again, lifting her head up with an expression now determined and resolute. 'Regrets are much worse than heartache. You do know that, Jamie? You do understand?'

Before I could answer, she'd wandered over to the fence to call Stan back inside.

She followed me to the door but before I entered, I said, 'You are right, Freya will be sent back from her aunt's. I know that now, and I understand we can never back down against Vic.'

'I know, love,' she said graciously. 'Go on inside. Let's have a cup of tea.'

20

SOMEWHERE IN BELGIUM, 1944

As soon as he saw it, something about the farmhouse had spooked Callaghan. They came in from the south and the woods away to the north-west obscured the view of any approaching enemy forces, but there was more to it; there was something else about the house that made him uneasy.

He suspected the site had been the scene of a fierce firefight. Part of the pitched thatch roof had been burnt away and, as they drew closer, he saw pockmarks from bullets in the beige brickwork and all but one of the small brown-framed windows had been shot through.

'What's wrong, Bill?' Baxter asked.

'Don't know, there's something about the place.'

'It looks deserted,' Baxter said, pushing through a broken gate, 'and we won't find somewhere else before dark. I think we should stay the night.'

'I know,' Callaghan agreed. 'Just keep your wits about you.'

Both men took out their handguns as they entered. They found a kitchen to one side of the house, with a black cast-iron stove and a pine table without chairs. A central staircase divided the kitchen from an empty living space with a brick fireplace built into the far wall.

They climbed the stairs to an open first floor divided only by a number of timber support struts. The upper floor had also been stripped bare and it lay empty except for a handful of dead pigeons that must have come in through a broken window or the damaged roof.

Baxter went outside and gathered some wood, and after he'd lit the stove, he made drinks while Callaghan perched on the table. Following a supper of tea and canned food and biscuits from their ration packs, they moved upstairs, set up beds from their groundsheets and fell into a deep, exhausted sleep.

Callaghan slept through until morning, when he woke with a start as somebody gripped and rocked his arm. He opened his eyes to find Baxter hunched over with a finger pressed to his lips.

'Downstairs,' Baxter whispered, 'there's somebody downstairs.'

Callaghan sat up. 'One of ours?' he asked quietly.

'Don't know.'

Callaghan extended his head around to the window, fearing the sight of a retreating German battalion. He breathed again when he saw the yard and fields beyond deserted except for the long morning shadows cast from the house.

A creak from a wooden stair tread turned him around. He saw a handgun and a soldier creeping up the staircase and he knew from the colour of uniform and the Walther P38 gun, he was the enemy.

The Wehrmacht soldier reacted at the sight of them, and he shaped to shoot.

Baxter had remained kneeling over and Callaghan pushed him violently out of the way, making his legs flip up as his torso fell backwards. The P38 fired and Callaghan went for his Enfield. As he picked up the rifle, he heard Baxter cry out in pain.

Still lying down, Callaghan fired the rifle. The bullet caught the German at the base of the neck and the force propelled him backwards and he landed at the top of the stairs.

Baxter writhed on the floor and clutched at his leg.

Callaghan went to speak, but an object dropped on the floorboards with a thud. He swivelled to his left and stared at the unmistakable sight of a German stick grenade.

He launched himself at it, and in one movement picked up the stick end and hurled it at the nearest window. The grenade caught the top left corner of the frame, but there was enough momentum to carry it outside, where it exploded.

Callaghan lurched back to his groundsheet and gathered up his rifle. As he had anticipated, a second soldier appeared on the staircase. The soldier swung around to shoot his pistol, but Callaghan squeezed the trigger and shot him in the chest. The impact of the bullet knocked the German off balance, and he lost his footing and skidded down the stairs.

Baxter had dragged himself to the Sten. He picked it up and in a strained voice, he said, 'There could be more of them, Bill.'

Callaghan grabbed two grenades from his satchel and

took the Sten from Baxter. When he reached the top of the stairs, he tossed the grenades down to the far end of the house. After they had exploded in quick succession, he stepped over the dead solider and charged down with the Sten.

Much to his relief, there were no other soldiers downstairs or outside. The soldier at the bottom of the stairs lay face down, his arm twitching. Callaghan picked up the Walther P38, that had been thrown under the kitchen table, and he stuck it in his belt. After checking the German had no other weapons, he returned upstairs.

'All clear down there,' he said to Baxter. 'Let's get out of here while we can. Can you walk?'

'It's not too bad,' Baxter replied. He had managed to stand and was leaning over to inspect the wound through a tear in his bloodstained trousers. 'It's just a nick across the top of the knee. Stings like hell but the bullet only grazed it. I can walk.'

'Are you losing blood?'

'A bit, but I can patch it up quickly.'

'Alright, do that now and then we'll get out of here,' Callaghan said, handing back the Sten. 'We can find somewhere quiet to strap it up properly.'

Baxter took out his knife, cut away a strip of his shirt sleeve, and tied it around his leg to stem the bleeding while Callaghan collected up their bags. The two Englishmen went downstairs to find the German had turned himself over, and he lay there staring at them wide-eyed as they descended.

Callaghan examined the young soldier's emaciated face. He got the impression it had aged prematurely, and although he could have passed for much older, Callaghan guessed he must be in his early 20s.

The German had unbuttoned his coat and from what Callaghan could see, the bullet had struck him below the shoulder. It had evidently missed all vital organs, but the extent of deep-red soaked into the shirt indicated a massive loss of blood.

The German lifted a shaking arm, and the sleeve of his oversized lieutenant's jacket slipped down as he did so. In his hand, he held a picture. He offered it to Callaghan, who hesitated, but reluctantly took the small crumpled black–and–white photo.

A young girl with a slender face, long flowing hair and a broad smile stared up at Callaghan. He nodded to acknowledge her, held the photo for Baxter to see, and then put it back in the young German's faltering hand.

'Freda,' the soldier managed to say, followed by something else Callaghan couldn't understand.

'What do we do, Bill?' Baxter asked.

'I don't know,' Callaghan said, and he thought over their options before finally shaking his head. 'We've got to go,' he said, and he led the way out through the front door. 'Let's get over by those trees and dress your leg.'

The two men walked briskly across the courtyard. When Callaghan climbed over a dilapidated wooden fence, the Walther pistol in his belt stuck in his stomach. He removed the gun and paused. 'We should go back,' he said. 'We can't let him die slowly.'

Callaghan ran back to the farmhouse and Baxter limped behind, and they found the soldier had hauled himself to the side of the stairs. He held the picture of Freda, and he gradually lifted his head.

Callaghan stood over him, holding the P38 pistol.

After jamming the gun in his belt, Callaghan crouched down and took out a picture of Betty, standing in front of the lake in Regent's Park.

The young German forced a weak smile and gently patted the top of Callaghan's arm.

Callaghan fed him some water from his canister, and he said slowly and clearly, 'We'll take you with us. There are Americans close by and they will have doctors.'

It was evident the German hadn't understood, but Callaghan motioned to Baxter, who helped pick up the wounded soldier. They put his arms around their shoulders and he screeched with pain as they lifted him to his feet.

At first, he hobbled with them, but by the time they'd taken him halfway across the courtyard, the German had stopped walking and Callaghan and Baxter were supporting his full weight as his feet dragged through the gravel.

'Let's put him down for a minute,' Baxter said breathlessly when they arrived at the fence. They lowered his body down and when they let go of his shoulders, he flopped back limply.

'He's dead, Bill,' Baxter said quietly.

Callaghan removed the photo of Freda from the soldier's pocket, put it in his lifeless hand, and draped his arms across his chest.

'Let's sort out your knee,' Callaghan said, and as he moved away from the body, he resisted the urge to look back.

When they stopped, they cleaned and dressed Baxter's leg with a clean bandage, cut from the sleeve of Callaghan's shirt.

Callaghan sat back against a tree and decided against

breakfast. He felt numb and wasn't hungry. His mind raced with thoughts of what might have been, and when he heard the sound of a vehicle engine, it came as a welcome diversion.

'They're Yanks,' Baxter called out, and he jumped to his feet and waved his arms.

Callaghan got up to see the white star on the front of the truck as it turned and drove towards them. Callaghan and Baxter walked out of the trees as the Jeep pulled up at their side.

The driver was huge with a sunburnt face and close-cropped red-brown hair, and he said in a strong accent, 'Hey, there, you guys need a ride?'

'We've been sent to find Major Turnbull,' Callaghan said. 'Can you take us to him?'

'We certainly can,' said the driver. 'He's the man who sent us out here. We've been looking for you. Hop in.'

Baxter climbed into the back seat and shoved over as Callaghan followed.

'I'm Sam, by the way,' the driver said. 'Sam Johnson from Austin, Texas.'

'And I'm Rodriguez,' said the skinny passenger, who twisted around to talk to them. 'You look like shit, man. What the hell's happened to you?'

Callaghan and Baxter introduced themselves and slumped back in their seats as the Jeep bumped its way through a series of fields. Rodriquez explained the retreat had long since passed and Sam Johnson talked mostly about oil and horses and his farmstead back home.

When they got to the American camp, Callaghan and Baxter reported to Major Turnbull. He told them a new radio had been dispatched by Jeep to Captain Douglas-Sykes earlier that morning along with Maynard and Hinchcliffe, but that he'd seen nothing of the other pairs who'd been sent out, although he promised to continue searching for them. He went on to confirm they were holding position for the rest of the day, but Johnson and Rodriquez would take them back to their battalion at 0600 the next morning.

Sam Johnson greeted them when they returned from Turnbull's tent. 'Hey, take this,' he said, and he pressed a bottle into Callaghan's hand. 'You look like you need it.'

Callaghan unscrewed the bottle and took a swig before handing it to Baxter.

'We're fixing up a card game,' Sam added. 'Why don't you get yourselves some food and then come and join us.'

'Bax needs a doctor, and I've got a letter to write,' Callaghan said, 'but when we're done, we'll take you up on that.' He turned away but swung back. 'And, Sam, thanks for the Scotch, it's decent stuff.'

Johnson laughed. 'That's not Scotch, Callaghan, that's Bourbon, Kentucky Bourbon. Go write your letter. When you're done, come on back and we'll deal you in. We'll drink a couple of bottles together but do yourself a favour, don't call it Scotch in front of the guys.'

Callaghan and Baxter left the group to find the doctor. When they saw the tent with a red cross, they separated. Callaghan said, 'I'm going to write a letter to Betty.'

'Alright, Bill,' Baxter said. 'I'll come and find you. Hey, Bill?'

'Yeah?'

'I thought I was going to die. Back there in the house when he shot at me, I thought that was it.'

'Not today, Larry,' Callaghan said. 'It wasn't your time, not today.'

Baxter turned to the tent, but Callaghan called him back. 'I almost forgot,' he said. 'I got you this.' He threw an object at Baxter, who caught it.

Larry Baxter peered down at the small cylindrical clock in his hand.

'I pulled it out of the Messerschmitt for you,' Callaghan said. 'It's for your repair shop. It's not working, but I thought you could fix it.'

21

THATCHAM, ENGLAND, 1986

A flurry of activity ensued and, one by one, preparations for the Friday-night attack on Vic fell into place.

After school on Thursday, Nan perched on the stool under the stairs as she phoned Sita. The call lasted 13 minutes. She deliberately kept her voice down and her mouth close to the receiver. I tried to eavesdrop, laid out flat on the landing at the top of stairs, but I couldn't make out more than a dozen or so words which, in isolation, made no sense.

After she'd finished, I went downstairs and ambled into the kitchen. Picking up the kettle, I casually asked, 'What's happening this weekend?'

Unsurprisingly, her response didn't give much away, but I detected a slight tension in her voice that wasn't usually there. 'Not a lot, love,' she said, as she rolled out some pastry. 'Why do you ask?'

Sita arrived in person at 6:25pm. I recognised her knock

and observed while stood over the draining board, drying the evening's washing-up. Aunty Flo opened the door, stepped outside for a few seconds, before returning and pulling the door to.

'Was that Sita?' I asked Aunty Flo as she tried to slip past me on her way back to the lounge. 'Why didn't she come in?'

'How did you know it was Sita?' she asked suspiciously.

'By her knock, she always knocks before coming in.'

'I suppose she does,' Aunty Flo conceded before turning away.

'So why didn't she come in?' I persisted, raising my voice a little so she couldn't ignore the question.

'She's busy. She had to get home.'

'What did she want, then?'

'Nothing much.'

'She must have wanted something?' I asked, determined not to let her off easily.

'You're a bit bloody nosey tonight, aren't you,' Aunty Flo said.

'It's just a bit odd; she normally comes in.'

'Well, if you must know, she dropped by to give me back some money she owes me,' Aunty Flo lied, 'but she had to zip off, because she's going to the bingo tonight. Is that alright by you?'

'Fine,' I said, 'just asking, that's all.'

With a disapproving glare, Aunty Flo departed for the lounge and left me in the kitchen alone.

I wandered over to the dining room window, drying the last bowl with a damp tea towel. I watched Sita scurry away up Paynesdown Road with her black umbrella set against the wind and sleeting rain. At the time, I very much doubted she really was heading to the bingo but looking back now, I know she had everything she needed to play her part the following night.

Preparations continued with another meeting late that night after I'd gone to bed. Larry arrived after midnight. Nan, Flo and Neil hadn't come up to bed and, from my position at the top of the stairs, I heard the four of them reconvene around the dining room table.

As I prepared to slither downstairs, the hallway door brushed opened, and Neil marched up toward me to use the toilet. I rolled over and fell back into my room and as I did so, it occurred to me how easily I might have been discovered loitering at the hallway door during their last session.

I waited for Neil to finish and return downstairs and then I descended myself but, as a precaution, I decided to hide by the telephone under the stairs. I couldn't hear as well from there, but it gave me a good chance of remaining undetected if somebody else used the toilet.

Crawling into position and wedging myself in between the phone table and the underside of the stairs, I heard Larry speak.

I hadn't noticed it before, and I suspect it was due to his partial deafness in one ear, but he tended to raise his voice and I heard him quite clearly. 'Are you absolutely certain she's not there?' he said. 'We've got to abort if there is any chance that she is.'

I realised he must be talking about Freya, but I couldn't pick out any of the muffled replies.

It seemed pointless to remain under the stairs if I couldn't hear anything. I squeezed out from the niche and moved closer to the door. I was now fully exposed, but I planned to dart back into position if I detected any suggestion that one of them needed a trip upstairs.

I heard Aunty Flo. 'I'm as certain as I can be,' she said after something that escaped me.

'Are you definitely sure it will work, Neil?' Larry said. 'Are you one hundred per cent certain?'

'Come on, Larry,' Aunty Flo said, 'we've been over this time and time again. Neil has already said it'll work. That is right, isn't it, dear? It will definitely work?'

Neil replied but he spoke quietly, and I didn't hear what he said. I pressed my ear hard up against the timber of the door, but he'd already finished.

'Larry, you don't need to be part of this, love,' Nan said, her words soothing and in contrast to the tetchy voices preceding it. 'You don't owe us anything. We're asking an awful lot, and we won't think any worse of you if you want to stay out of it.'

'No, it's not that, Bet,' Larry said. 'I just want to be certain, that's all. I'm in. I'm in all the way, whatever it takes.'

Nan then took control. She revealed the full extent of the plan, step by step, and issued individual instructions to each member of the team. I listened in astonishment.

'Right, that's it,' Nan said emphatically, 'we're on. We go tomorrow; it's now or never.'

The meeting began to break up and, wary one of them could burst through the door at any moment, I withdrew back to my room and eased the door silently into its jamb.

Bewildered by what I had heard, I didn't sleep. The next

morning, I considered feigning illness to avoid school, but I reasoned stewing at home all day with nothing to do would have been even worse than going in and doing something to occupy my mind.

After a slow morning, I found a quiet spot in the corner of the library at lunchtime with a view out across the tennis courts. The early morning downpours had passed, but the concrete remained damp and the overcast skies of charcoal grey hung low and threatened to open up again at any moment.

A fight broke out on the field beyond the tennis courts and a swarm of kids gathered round into a closed huddle. Two teachers from the music block eventually appeared and pushed through to put a stop to it and disperse the crowd.

The football match on the courts resumed. A group of girls heckled from the side as the boys rushed after the ball and pushed and pulled at each other's coats.

I envied them. It was the last day of term, and they all had the Christmas break to look forward to. My future seemed so uncertain in comparison. It was at that exact moment I decided I had to act. I couldn't stay in my room that night and simply hope for the best.

My thoughts returned to the dingy, seedy casino in amongst the filthy streets of Soho. Billy Apple's words came back to me. He had said, 'If you're ever in danger, kid, run towards it and meet it head on,' and that is what I intended to do.

When I got home, I found Nan stood at the lounge window, smoking a cigarette and flicking the ash into the heavy cut-glass ashtray she held in front of her at waist level. Deep in thought, she hadn't heard me come in the back door.

A sad song played softly on the radio, and I watched her for a moment without her knowing.

The deeply wrinkled skin on the back of her hand revealed her age and each time she raised her hand to draw from her cigarette, I thought I detected a slight tremor.

'Oh, hello, love,' she said, when she at last did notice me. 'It's cheese on toast for tea. Don't expect anything special tonight.'

'That's fine,' I replied. 'Where's Aunty Flo? Has she gone out?'

'No, she's up in her room. She's not feeling that great.'

'What's wrong?' I asked. 'It's not like her?'

'She's got a migraine, so be quiet when you go up.'

I switched on the TV while Nan cleared out and cleaned the cabinet in the dining room. She'd been threatening to do it for months and I guessed she wanted to keep busy as the clock ticked slowly over.

Neil got back late from work and by the time he returned home, Nan and I had finished our dinner. I thought he looked paler than he usually did, and, for the first time, I noticed he had dark bags sagging beneath his staring eyes.

His jacket fell from its peg behind the door, but he managed to hang it up at the second attempt. From the dining room table, where I sat reading through the local paper, I pretended not to notice his skittish movements around the kitchen.

He removed a glass from the cupboard and went to fill it with milk, before deciding against it and putting the bottle of milk back in the fridge.

'What's wrong with her?' he asked, unable to hide his concern when Nan told him Aunty Flo was in her room.

'She'll be fine, love,' Nan said, sliding his cheese on toast under the grille. 'She's just gone for a lie-down. It's nothing to worry about.'

Neil eventually came and sat down next to me, where he picked silently at his toast. He didn't stay long, and with half of his tea uneaten, he made excuses about finishing off some paperwork and he went upstairs.

'I'm going to finish off clearing out the unit,' Nan said when he'd gone.

Aunty Flo and Neil didn't appear again, so I ended up spending the evening alone in front of the TV with only the dogs for company.

I struggled to find something to watch but I eventually found a sitcom I liked, although it wasn't as funny as I remembered. After that, I persevered for as long as I reasonably could with a film about a bank robbery before I finally lost interest and switched off the TV.

'I'm going up, Nan,' I said through the kitchen arch as she crouched down in front of the cabinet.

'Alright, love, I'll be up soon.'

I kissed her cheek and gave her a hug, and I tried not to hang on for any longer than I usually did.

In the hope I'd get some sleep before the time came, I set the alarm on my digital watch to 02:45am. I knew my watch alarm would wake me but be quiet enough that nobody else would hear it.

At 02:37am I cancelled the alarm having not slept.

For hours I'd stared at the ceiling and listened to the familiar groans and creaks that our house made in the dead of night. But now, it began to stir. I heard light switches click on and off and floorboards gently squeak. Three pairs of feet then cascaded down the stairs in sequence, and they failed to dodge the noisy treads that I'd trained myself to avoid with years of practice.

Larry must have been waiting at the back door. It creaked open.

I quickly dressed in the clothes I'd carefully laid out a few hours before and I tiptoed into Nan's bedroom. From the window, I realised they hadn't let Larry in, but the others had immediately stepped outside to join him.

Driving forward against the wind, Larry led the way across the road, followed by Nan and Aunty Flo. Neil closed our gate behind him when he passed through it.

I bolted downstairs and checked the kitchen junk drawer for the torch. It wasn't there.

With their laces already tied, I pinched my fingertips as I hastily pulled on my trainers.

Getting to my feet, I leant on the kitchen counter to check what was happening outside through the slot window at the end of the kitchen.

Larry had separated from the others. He'd gone to the front of Vic's house. He peered in through the lounge window, his hands raised up either side of his eyes and pressed against the glass.

He motioned to Nan and Aunty Flo, who were waiting by Vic's car, and they closed in on the back door.

Neil had stayed at the gate. He checked up and down Bourne Road and then over the crossroads, where he stretched to see as far as he could up Paynesdown Road.

Nan reached Vic's back door, but then Aunty Flo obscured my view of her. Aunty Flo fished in the handbag hanging at her side, suspended by a strap over her shoulder.

She drew a key. From the conversation I'd overheard during their first meeting, I knew they'd had a spare key cut two weeks before on a Thursday morning when Vic was at work and Freya had left for school.

From her bedroom window, Nan had often seen Freya leave the key under the pot. Nan had taken it, arranged for Larry to drive her into Reading to get a copy made, and replaced it before Freya returned home. They'd agreed it was safer to get the copy made in Reading rather than risk seeing somebody they knew getting it cut in Thatcham or Newbury.

Nan took the key from her sister and threaded it into the lock. She entered, followed closely by Aunty Flo and Larry, who had run around the house, and finally Neil, who had left his post as lookout.

As soon as they'd all disappeared out of sight, I made my move.

I slipped out the door and into the night.

22

A blustering wind swirled around our backyard, at first tossing my hair forward and then dragging it back from my forehead.

When I reached our gate, I lifted the latch and eased it open, being careful to raise it up on its hinges so the base didn't scrape against the concrete.

Beyond the line of conifers, with their branches swaying violently back and forth with each gust, a solitary soft-drink can rattled in the gutter of the deserted street.

I crossed the road. When on the other side, I slid past Vic's car to follow in Larry's footsteps around to the front of the house. To stay out of sight, I stooped down low with my palms pressing down on the dank grass for balance.

Further up Paynesdown Road, I thought I heard the murmur of faint voices. I stopped to listen, but I couldn't hear anything more against the howling wind.

I pressed up against the glass of Vic's lounge window.

The drawn curtains had caught on the windowsill and buckled into a crevice large enough for me to see through.

Lit by the glow of the TV, Vic's body lay sprawled out on the settee, eyes closed, mouth open, with one arm drooping downwards and the other neatly folded across his chest.

At the base of the sofa by Vic's dangling hand, an empty can of beer turned over on its side sat next to the TV remote control, which must have fallen as its two batteries had broken loose and scattered across the floor.

Then I saw it, the very thing that everything hinged upon. An empty plate lay on the coffee table at the end of the sofa with a used knife and fork resting on it. He'd gone for it and for the first time, I thought the plan might actually work. Vic had eaten the drugged curry Sita had cooked and delivered to him earlier that night.

The shadowy figures of Nan and Aunty Flo entered and circled around the settee. Nan shone the torch, directing its beam up and down Vic's body and around the room while Aunty Flo hovered directly above him. Aunty Flo removed a small brown pot of pills with a white cap from her bag.

Nan held the torch in place while Aunty Flo crouched down and pressed the pot up against the fingertips of Vic's loose hand. She wore a pair of shiny black gloves, and, at the second attempt, she pushed down to twist the cap off the pot before placing both next to the empty can of beer.

The tablets had been discussed during their first meeting.

'They're bloody awful things,' Aunty Flo had said, 'but a guy from the Barley Mow in Hayling Island got them for me when I was struggling with Conor.'

'Why? What happened?' asked Neil.

'It's a story for another day, Neil, but it was a bad time for all of us. I got myself in a bit of a state and I was pretty desperate. I tried everything else, but those tablets were the only way I could get some sleep.'

'So, they must be well out of date?' Nan asked.

'Oh, God, yeah,' Aunty Flo said, 'but I tried half of one on Sunday night and, bloody hell, it knocked me out in minutes. They still work alright, and they still make you groggy as hell the next day. Horrible things. I don't have enough left to kill the bastard, but they'll knock him out alright.'

Listening from behind the door, I had heard Larry clear his throat. 'But can they be traced back to you, Florence?'

Larry's concern was evident from the way he spoke, and his use of 'Florence' instead of 'Flo' struck me as odd.

'No chance,' Aunty Flo reassured him, 'this guy used to get them from a mate of his who lived in Florida.'

'But the police could make the connection?' Larry said.

'No way, it was years ago and although he was dishing them out to loads of people, everything was kept hush-hush.'

Nan joined in, 'But what if the police have busted this guy since you last saw him?'

'They haven't,' Aunty Flo replied. 'The last time I saw him he was in a wooden box being lowered into the ground. He croaked it not long after all this happened. His heart packed up on him. He used to get all sorts of other tablets. He was one of these muscle-man bodybuilder types and in the end, all the tablets he used did him in. He was only 37.'

Larry and Neil came into view through the crack in the curtain. Larry paced up and down behind the sofa, rubbing his chin as he examined Vic's body. I couldn't hear, but Nan spoke to Neil, and he nodded in reply.

When the wind died down, I detected voices in the

street again. They were closer, much closer, and there was no doubt in my mind now they were coming my way.

'Don't think I'm bloody stupid,' I heard a woman say.

'What? I couldn't help it,' a man slurred back. 'She started talking to me. What could I do?'

Back at the window, the four dark figures gathered around Vic. Nan held the torch in one hand, but she now had a bottle of vodka or possibly gin in the other.

There had been no mention of a bottle of liquor during their meetings and I couldn't be entirely certain where it had come from.

Larry and Neil closed in on Vic's upper torso, each digging their hands down under his shoulders ready to prise him off the settee while Aunty Flo picked up his legs.

'I couldn't tell her to fuck off, could I?' the drunken man continued to protest.

The arguing couple had almost reached me. A caravan parked in the garden next door obscured their view, but any second, they would be past it and they would see me.

I tore myself away from the window and dropped to my knees behind the garden hedge.

'Yes, you should have told her to fuck off,' the woman scolded. 'That's exactly what you should have done.'

'Don't be ridiculous,' the man replied. 'Look, I'm sorry, I won't speak to her again, OK?'

'You said that last time. You treat me like I'm some kind of idiot.'

Damp from the grass seeped through the knees of my trousers. The couple were immediately above me now. I waited for them to pass, but instead, the woman's footsteps stopped. Low down through the branches of the hedge, I saw her two small-heeled red shoes at a standstill and a pair of pristine white trainers with blue stripes that had walked on.

'No, I don't. Come on, I'm sorry, alright?' the man pleaded.

With a change of tone, the woman whispered, 'Did you see that?'

'See what? Come on, I've said I'm sorry. I can't do anymore.'

'Look, in there, did you see it?' the woman repeated.

'See what?'

'Look, in that window. There it is again.'

'What? I can't see anything.'

'Steve,' the woman snapped, 'in that window, that one, there's somebody in there.'

'So what?' the man slurred back.

'But they've got a torch. Why would they have a torch?'

'It's nothing. They've probably just got a power cut.'

'No, they don't. Look, there's a light on up there in that window. It looks like a burglary.'

'Hey, come on, you don't know that.'

'Look, there it is. You can see the torch,' the woman hissed. 'You know Stacey, at my work, she lives over in Crowfield Drive and she got burgled three weeks ago. Four houses in the same street, all got done the same night. Come on, we're calling the police. We'll use the phone box at the top of the road.'

Their footsteps hurried away at a jogging pace.

I climbed to my feet to see them turn the corner at the crossroads, the woman ahead of the man and dragging at his arm.

The wind blew up Paynesdown Road and sent the discarded soft-drink can tumbling. Its hollow clatter echoed around the empty street.

I made up my mind quickly. As I saw it, I had no choice. I had to warn Nan the police were coming. After sprinting around Vic's house, I took a deep breath and slowly turned the door handle to let myself in.

23

The light from the torch burned my eyes.

'Jamie, get home now,' Nan rapped, 'this is no place for you.'

'But you've got to listen to me.'

'No, Jamie,' Nan said firmly. 'You go home now, and you forget what you've seen here. Do you hear me?'

She lowered the torch, allowing my eyes to adjust. In the dim second-hand light from a street lamp, I saw that Larry, Neil and Aunty Flo had dragged Vic's body from the lounge, through the kitchen and halfway into the dining room, but each of the figures before me had frozen into statues when I'd walked in.

'Please listen,' I said again, more desperately this time. 'The police are coming.'

'No, they're not,' Nan snapped. 'Jamie, I'm not going to tell you again. You have got to go home now.'

'Yes, they are. The police will be here soon. Two people walking home saw the torch through the window. They think it's a burglary and they've gone to call 999. I heard them.'

'Jamie,' Aunty Flo said, her back still hunched over as she held onto Vic's legs. 'I'm going to swear now, because this is no time for you to start fucking about.'

'I'm being serious. Please believe me. They've gone to the phone box at the top of the road.'

Aunty Flo let go of Vic's ankles and straightened. 'He's telling the truth, Bet. What do we do?'

A white-faced clock high up on the wall at the end of the kitchen ticked over loudly as we waited for Nan to respond. It felt as though each tick might be its last, but it doggedly kept on going.

'Jamie,' Nan said finally, 'how long ago did you hear them?'

'Just now, just a few seconds ago.'

'Heading to the phone box up by the shop?'

'Yes,' I said.

'How much do you know?'

'Everything. I overheard your meeting in the dining room.'

I thought she'd be furious, but I should have known better. There was plenty of time for that later, but it wasn't important now. Instead of telling me off, she gave me orders. 'Shoes off and go in there,' she said, pointing to the lounge. 'Keep watch from the window and let us know if the police arrive. Stay out of sight behind the curtain and do not let them see you. Understood?'

I nodded and ran past her to the lounge. Nan shouted, 'Go!' to the others, and they resumed pulling Vic's body.

I went past the sofa and gripped the top of the radiator under the window. It was still lukewarm, and it warmed my hands while I took in the view outside through the opening in the curtains. The angle of the crevice restricted my line of sight, so I adjusted it to reveal a better view of the crossroads.

I began to shiver. With nothing to do but gaze out into an empty street, the nerves I'd managed to suppress while running around outside returned and were made worse by the scraping and banging and rasping voices coming from the dining room.

As the noises in the other room grew, the temptation to see what was happening became unbearable. I planned to take a quick look before coming straight back to my post, but by the time I was halfway across the lounge, headlights flashed across the room. A car had swung around the crossroads.

I quickly returned to the window and tightened the gap in the curtains to a sliver.

The car had passed by, but I could still make out the hum of its engine. Moments later, it crawled into view. Having turned around, a white car with 'Police' written down the side in large blue letters pulled up to a standstill in front of Vic's house. The siren didn't sound, but the beacon on the roof switched on and bathed the street in a rotating blue light. Both front doors flung open.

A sharp pain pierced the sole of my foot as I dashed across the lounge. I'd trodden on one of the batteries from the TV remote control. Limping into the dining room, I found it exactly as Freya had explained, a mirror image of ours but with a disabled bathroom cut out of the far corner. A smudge of blue pulsating light from the police car crept in around the edges of the closed curtains.

Through the open bathroom door and the crowd around him, I saw that Vic had been stripped naked and hauled into the bath through the disabled access door panel.

Some water had been drawn into the bath, but the taps were now shut off.

Vic's head, resting on the back of the bath at the opposite end to the taps, swung from side to side and his eyes fluttered open as he tried to speak.

Neil, with feet in the bath and water up to his ankles, leant over Vic to pin his shoulders down while Aunty Flo held his nose and both Nan and Larry tried to force the bottle of vodka or gin down his throat to subdue him.

I gasped. 'The police are here.'

'You think we don't know that?' Aunty Flo hissed as she pointed to the pulse of blue light at the window.

'Jamie,' Nan said, more calmly than I thought possible, 'is the back door locked? You've got to stay out of sight and make sure it's locked.'

Leaving the struggle behind, I closed the bathroom door and crawled across the dining room carpet to the kitchen.

The front doorbell rang, followed by a loud knock, and an even louder, 'Open up, it's the police.'

A second heavy thud on the door sent a shudder through me, but it also brought a sense of relief. If the police were at the front of the house, I had time to lock the back door.

'Stop him, stop him,' I heard Nan say in a subdued cry from the bathroom, before something, possibly a bottle of shampoo, slapped onto the floor.

The sound of radio interference confused me. It appeared to come from the rear of the house, and a deep male voice with a broad Welsh accent spoke after it.

From my position lying flat on the kitchen floor, I watched a tall policeman with a bushy beard walk past the kitchen window towards the back door.

I'd misread the situation, and I now realised the two officers had split up. One had approached the front while the other went around to the rear, and the latter was seconds away from barging in the back door.

Behind me, a commotion broke out in the bathroom and what I assumed to be a flailing arm smashed into a wall before splashing down into water.

Staying close to the tiled kitchen floor, I scrambled to the door. I fumbled for the key, turned it over in its lock, and winced at the noise the latching mechanism made as it clicked into place.

Background noise from his radio cut in and out and the tall policeman banged on the frosted-glass panel. 'It's the police!' he shouted through the door.

I curled up into a ball at the base of the door, praying he couldn't see me, and praying the noise from the radio had masked the sound of the key locking.

The glass shook in its frame as he thumped it repeatedly for a second time. The handle twisted but the locked door held firm as the officer pushed up against it.

Another clamour came from the bathroom. I pictured Vic coming out of his stupor to thrash around in the water. The disturbance climaxed with a thunderous slap on the wall.

Any remaining hope I had that we would get away with Vic's murder now drained out of me.

The Welsh officer must have heard the fracas, and I held my breath, waiting for his reaction.

Our luck had run out. Deep down I'd thought the plan was destined to fail but being proved right brought no consolation.

Soon the house would be surrounded by police cars and one by one, the five of us would be handcuffed and driven away up Paynesdown Road.

I eventually opened my eyes and craned my neck around to see what was happening outside.

Through the obscured glass, I saw the murky figure of the tall officer. He'd stepped away from the door, further into the garden, and he held his radio up to his ear.

Ambling around casually, he appeared to be looking up at the windows on the floor above, whilst occasionally shaking, and then returning the radio to his ear.

Nothing in his movements suggested he'd just called in a suspicious incident.

Could it be possible he hadn't heard anything? The noise from the bathroom had been so loud it was hard to believe he didn't hear it, and I could only guess the noise from his radio had blocked it out.

There seemed to be a persistent problem with his radio receiver, and as he came closer to the house, I could again hear bursts of broken interference while he tinkered with its knobs and buttons.

The second officer, fatter and shorter in silhouette, joined him at the back of the house and they exchanged words. The shorter man removed his radio from its clip and spoke into it, before the pair disappeared from view and walked around to the front.

With a sense of renewed hope, I skidded across the kitchen tiles to the lounge. Before I made it to the window, a car door slammed shut, followed by the second, and the blue flashing light switched off. The engine revved up and the police car drove away.

I went to the bathroom and tugged the door open. 'They've gone,' I said, as water wet my feet.

Vic lay writhing in the middle of the room with his four attackers above, battling to overpower him. He wasn't fully conscious, but he'd come round enough to unlock the bath access door, open it, and force his way out.

Upon hearing my words, Nan shouted, 'Come on, we can take him now!'

Neil thrust his knee down on Vic's left shoulder. He cried out in pain which allowed Aunty Flo to wedge his mouth open with the handle of a hairbrush. Nan, holding the bottle of what I could now see was vodka, delicately tipped up the bottle to trickle its contents into the corner of Vic's open mouth.

Larry, using his knees like the two grips of a vice, locked Vic's head into place, and Vic had no option but to gulp for breath while the dribble of liquor rolled down his throat.

'Hold him steady,' Nan said each time Vic's body shuddered, and the bottle soon emptied.

Vic's body went limp. His eyes briefly blinked open and rolled over, but they closed again as his head slumped over to one side.

'Get him back in there,' Nan barked.

Larry, Neil and Aunty Flo heaved his bulk through the access door into the bath.

When his body was in position, Aunty Flo closed and locked the door and turned on the hot and cold taps simultaneously.

'What the hell are you doing?' she asked when Neil picked up a bottle of bubble bath from the shelf. 'Do you want me to go home and get him a rubber duck to play with as well?'

'No, Florence,' Nan said, 'he's right. Go on, love, tip some in. It's got to look like an accident, remember. He's taking a bath like he always would.'

Neil poured in a good measure and the water bubbled up.

I then noticed, for the first time, Neil was wearing transparent cellophane gloves, as were Nan and Larry.

'You've got to go in the other room now, love,' Nan said to me. 'You can't be here for the next bit. Go on into the lounge. We'll go home together when we're done. Keep a look out in case the police come back. Before you go, take your socks off and dry your feet with that towel. Don't leave any wet footprints around.'

'I haven't got gloves,' I said. 'I've left fingerprints on the door and the key and maybe in some other places I can't remember.'

'Doesn't matter,' she replied. 'A few fingerprints here and there from a young neighbour and a friend of Freya's aren't suspect, but leaving wet footprints after all this is a different story. Don't worry, go into the lounge and I'll come and get you soon.'

I took off my socks and dried my feet before backing out of the room and leaving the door ajar. With absolutely no intention whatsoever of going into the lounge, I ducked down and hid in the far corner of the room under the dining room table.

Neil came out after me and through the legs of the table and chairs, I watched him walk into the kitchen. He returned carrying the small grey portable TV with the cord and plug dragging behind.

Neil had left the bathroom door wide open and through it, I saw him precariously rest the TV on the corner of the bath next to the taps.

The white cord trailed out into the dining room. Neil tracked back after it, picked up the plug and slotted it into a double socket next to a pine storage cabinet. He said to the others, 'Stay well back, I'm turning it on,' and he flicked the socket switch into the on position.

Steam had by now filled the bathroom and through the fog I saw a shallow mound of white fluffy bubbles had risen up above the top of the bath.

'That's enough,' Nan said to Aunty Flo, who shut off the taps.

Neil joined the other three and they stood in a circle to discuss the next move.

Through a gap in the crowd, I thought I saw Vic's eyes flicker open.

I rubbed my tired eyes to look again, uncertain if they'd deceived me. They hadn't. Vic's head fell forward, and his eyes blinked again but the others hadn't noticed. He raised a shaky hand to push some of the bubbles next to his face to one side.

Larry faced away from me and I couldn't hear him, but he appeared to be leading the discussion. After waving the others back, he shifted over to take hold of the TV.

'Get ready,' Aunty Flo said, 'stand well back, Neil.'

Before Nan could step back, Vic rose up out of the bath and grabbed at her. Larry lunged forward to intercept but as he pushed off, he knocked into the TV.

I pictured events unfolding in my mind before they happened.

Larry cut across Vic, rescuing Nan as he pushed her to the floor, but Vic caught hold of him instead.

The TV dropped into the bath with a sizzling noise.

Aunty Flo screamed, 'No, Larry!' as Vic dragged him back and they both plunged into the water.

24

'Jamie!' Nan cried out. 'Don't move.'

Aunty Flo and Neil swung around to see me lying on the dining room floor, holding the TV plug I'd pulled out of the socket.

Soapy water spilled from the bath as Larry and Vic tussled.

Neil took two steps forward, stooped down, and swung at Vic.

The punch caught Vic square on the chin and his head snapped to one side. Neil struck him a second time and Vic released Larry, who awkwardly clambered out of the bath.

'Everybody out!' shouted Nan.

Aunty Flo, Neil and Larry bundled out of the room, leaving Vic behind in the bath. A soaking-wet Larry fell to his knees. Nan dropped to the floor, grabbed the plug out of my hand and rammed it in the socket.

A blaze of blue crackled in the bathroom and sparks erupted from the submerged TV.

Vic's body shuddered and fell back.

We watched Vic sink into the bubbles as wispy circles of smoke drifted up to the ceiling.

Nan kissed the top of my head and whispered in my ear, 'Well done,' but her business-like manner quickly returned. 'Right, we're not out of this yet,' she said. 'We need to move quickly. Larry, Neil, you two get Jamie home. Me and Florence will clean this place up and make sure we've not left anything. Dry yourselves off with this before you go.'

She handed Larry a towel from the bathroom.

'Keep your gloves on until you're home,' she continued, 'and be careful not to be seen. The police were out a few minutes ago and the whole street would have been rubbernecking. Check before you go and if the coast isn't clear, stay put until it is. Alright?'

Judging from his haunted expression, Larry appeared to be in shock. He puffed his cheeks out and held the towel up against his face.

Nan placed a hand on his upper arm. 'Are you alright, Larry?'

He lowered the towel, gave an unconvincing nod, and began to pat himself down to soak up the worst of the water.

'Don't forget,' Nan said as Larry, Neil and I made for the door, 'put all your clothes in the bag when you get back. You too, Jamie, Neil will show you.'

The three of us put our shoes on, sneaked out the door, and after Neil had scanned the neighbours' overlooking windows, we crept across the street.

The cold remained but the wind had died down, and when I looked for the discarded drinks can, it was nowhere to be seen.

25

After an agonising 20-minute wait, a blast of wintery air chased Nan and Aunty Flo in through our back door. Larry, Neil and I greeted them from the dining room table, where we'd gathered after getting changed.

Apart from the occasional "are you OK, Jamie?" from Neil, we'd sat in silence, each replaying the night's events over in our minds.

'Did you get back alright?' Nan asked through the kitchen arch. 'Nobody saw you?'

'No, definitely not,' Neil replied. 'All clear when we came over.'

'Good,' Nan said, 'same for us, all quiet.'

She dumped down two bin sacks, presumably full of wet towels and other incriminating items, and came over to the dining room window. She peeled back an inch of curtain and scanned the street.

'Fuck me,' Aunty Flo said. 'That was a close call, Bet. I'd forgotten how much fun you can be on a Friday night.'

'I've had worse Friday nights out with you,' Nan replied, and the two sisters lit cigarettes at the same time.

At the back of Neil's chair, Aunty Flo affectionately patted him on the shoulder. He'd changed into the pale-yellow pyjamas with a pair of fluffy bunny rabbits on the breast pocket she'd bought him for his birthday. 'Be a dear and get some drinks in,' she said. 'I think we all need one.'

'Get Bill's bourbon out, love,' Nan said, and she sat down at the head of the table.

Neil removed four glasses from the drinks' cabinet, set them on the table, and poured the bourbon.

'Get one for Jamie as well,' Nan said, 'just a small one, mind, but he deserves one.'

Nan picked up her glass, swirled the liquid around, and took a sip. 'You know full well you weren't supposed to be part of that,' she said to me, 'but the way things turned out, we're all glad you were.'

'Especially me,' Larry said. 'Thank you, Jamie. I thought I'd had it back there.'

It came as a relief to hear Larry speak; he'd barely said a word since Vic had dragged him into the bath.

'Your nan tells me you've read some of your grandad's letters from the war,' Larry went on, his voice a little unsteady. 'You might have read he once saved my life as well. He'd be proud of you, Jamie, if he was still here.'

'He would,' Nan said, 'and your mum and dad would be as well.' She placed her hand on mine and squeezed.

I drained my glass in one. The liquor burned through my chest and filled my stomach with a warm, comforting feeling.

'I know you overheard our meetings, love,' Nan said,

'but there are other things you need to know, to really understand why we did what we did tonight.'

'We only did it because we had to, Jamie,' Aunty Flo chimed in.

'And I can assure you,' Nan said, 'it wasn't something we took lightly.'

'What is it don't I know?' I asked.

'It all goes back years, love,' Nan began, 'long before you would remember. I once told you that Freya's mum died in an accident; well, that's not true. It wasn't an accident. Vic killed her. We suspect she found out what Vic, Meadows, and those other two were up to, and when she confronted him, he killed her.'

'What?' I interrupted. 'Does Freya know?'

'No, love,' Nan said. 'She was too young.'

'What were they up to? What did Freya's mum find out?'

'They're bad people, love. They've done a lot of bad things over the years. They're part of an organisation, an evil organisation that do nasty things to people who are different to them.'

'Why do they do it?'

'I don't know, love. I really don't know, but it broke your grandad's heart to have a vicious bastard like that living across the street, when he'd fought a war to keep racist scum out of our country. You won't find anything in his letters, and he never even mentioned it to me, but he saw some awful things during the war. Towards the end, he was separated from Larry, and he was there when they liberated Bergen-Belsen, so he knew better than anyone what men like Vic Dyson can do if you don't stand up to them.'

'What's Bergen-Belsen?' I asked.

'It was a concentration camp. A lot of innocent men, women and children were killed there, and he saw what they did to those poor people. I only know all of this because the nurses at the hospital told me. When they gave him electric-shock treatment, he told them things he'd never said to anyone else before, and he said things about losing your mum and dad as well. He couldn't cope with the grief on top of what he was already going through. But they thought his experience at Bergen-Belsen started his illness, and he found it so hard living with someone like Vic over the road. If he'd been well enough and 20 years younger, he would have sorted those bastards out himself, but even though they were always wary of him, the truth is, he was in no condition to do anything about them.'

I said, 'Vic's gang burned down Sita's flat, didn't they? And they attacked Larry?'

'Probably,' Nan replied. 'We don't know for certain, but yes, we suspect it was them. That's the kind of thing they would do, and they've done far worse than that over the years. And Meadows would always cover their tracks.'

'What happened to Freya's mum?'

Nan nodded to acknowledge the question but hesitated before answering. She finished the last of her drink and said, 'Sarah. That's what her name was, Sarah. She was a kind, gentle lady. Beautiful as well, and I expect Freya will look just like her when she's older. God knows why she ever got caught up with a bloke like that, and I'm sure she wouldn't have done if she'd known what he was really like. We suspect she found out about something they had done one day, and when she confronted him, there was this huge argument.'

'At their house, here?' I asked.

'Oh yeah, it all happened here. I remember it as if it was yesterday. It happened on a baking-hot Sunday evening. It was so hot we all had our windows open, so all the neighbours heard the row. It got so bad I ended up going over there with your grandad but we were too late. By the time we got there, we found her on the kitchen floor. She'd suffered a trauma to the back of the head. Vic was crouched down by her side, trying to work out what to do. At first, he told us to "piss off" but then, in a panic, he told us she'd fallen down the stairs; the lying bastard. She was in the middle of the kitchen, and he expected us to believe she'd fallen down the stairs, and he'd dragged her through the house?'

She shook her head at the memory. Neil held up the bottle of bourbon to offer more, and when Nan raised her eyebrows, he topped up her glass.

'Didn't you call the police?'

'Yes, yes of course we did,' Nan said, seemingly surprised at the question. 'We came straight back here and phoned them, but Sergeant Meadows arrived minutes later, and he was first on the scene. Vic must have called him first, and that was it, he covered everything up. Vic went in for questioning, but he was never charged. Me and your grandad tried everything to get the case properly investigated but Sergeant Meadows had so much sway, he was able to block our every move. We tried for years but Meadows was seen as a hero because he'd saved a couple of kids from drowning down the canal two or three years before. He got to go to Buckingham Palace and get a medal and all that. He was in the local paper all the time and people thought he could do no wrong, and nobody more senior wanted to question it when he covered things up.'

Everything was falling into place, and I said, 'Vic went to his retirement party the other day, didn't he?'

'That's right, love. From what we've heard, he's being forced to retire so he wouldn't be able to cover for them anymore. They tried to scare me off but when they realised I wouldn't back down and I would go to the police, they had to do something more drastic. When Freya told you that Vic was planning something for the 19th, it only confirmed our suspicions.'

'And that's why,' Aunty Flo said, 'we had to get him first.'

'But will Sergeant Meadows and the others come after us?' I asked.

'No chance,' Nan said emphatically. 'With Meadows retired and Vic out of the way, they won't do anything. Vic was their muscle; he was always the one who got his hands dirty. Those other cowards wouldn't dare try anything without him. They had one shot, but they blew it, and that chance has gone now.'

'But what about the police?' I asked. 'Won't they know that we did it? If the police question you, what will you say? Will you say you liked him?'

'I'll say I couldn't stand him,' Nan said. 'We obviously won't tell the police everything, but it would be suspicious to say we liked him when everyone around here knows full well we didn't. To be clear, Jamie, if the police ask you anything, you tell them the truth. We hide nothing that's happened in the past, we'll only get found out if we do. The only thing you don't mention is what happened tonight. You've been in bed all night. You didn't hear a thing. You didn't see a thing. The police car with the blue flashing light, you didn't see it. Nobody saw it, nobody saw it apart from me out of my bedroom window, and I told you all at breakfast the next day, alright?'

'But, Nan, when we tell them everything won't it make us look guilty?'

'No, not at all. Neighbours everywhere fall out, but it doesn't mean they kill each other, does it?'

'But—'

'Jamie,' Nan cut me off. 'Look around this table. What do you see? Do we look like a bunch of vicious murderers? A couple of frail old ladies, a limping old man, a 12-year-old schoolboy and young man in his bunny-rabbit pyjamas? How often do you see people like us plastered all over the newspapers? Look at these murdering villains. And what would they call us? The Paynesdown Road 5? People would never believe it, people would laugh.'

I looked around the table at the kind eyes staring back at me. Of course, she was right. It seemed obvious to me now. Aunty Flo grinned and held up her glass for Neil to top up.

We were the Paynesdown Road 5, but nobody would ever believe it.

'Let's drink up the last of Bill's bourbon,' Nan said. 'It's a good time to finish it.'

The wind outside whistled and rattled at the windows, and I lost all track of time as the five of us sat there, drinking, and exchanging glances without a word spoken.

'I'm sorry you all had to go through that tonight,' Nan said, to finally break the silence, 'but thank you for everything.'

A wave of tiredness suddenly washed over me, and I struggled to keep my eyes open, but it was Aunty Flo who spoke up before I did.

'Well, that's me for the night, Bet,' she said, getting to her feet. 'If anyone wants the bathroom, you better be quick. I think I fancy a bath.'

She laughed at her own joke, downed her bourbon, and disappeared upstairs without saying goodnight.

26

'To be perfectly honest,' Nan said, as she leant on the gate with one hand and held a cigarette in the other. 'I despised the bloke. Couldn't stand him.'

I nudged open the bathroom window a touch further to see Mrs Higgins on the other side of the fence. Higgins looked as though she would say something, but Nan went on, 'Don't get me wrong, it's sad Freya has lost both her parents, but it was when her mum died, that was the real tragedy. I'm sure you agree?'

'Oh yes,' the podgy old woman replied, clearly desperate to say her piece. 'We all knew that you hated him and you're absolutely right about Sarah. She was a lovely lady. If you ask me, and lots of people do, there was something a bit fishy about the way she died.'

'Yes, that's right, I remember you saying so at the time,' Nan said, pointing her cigarette at Mrs Higgins in agreement. 'Didn't you say all four of them were up to no good? Vic, Sergeant Meadows and those other two that used to go round there?'

'Oh yes,' Higgins said excitedly. She put down her two shopping bags in preparation for a long conversation. 'They're wrongun's, the lot of them. I always knew they were bad news. I've been saying so for years, but nobody would listen to me, nobody would ever do anything about it.'

'And now Vic's dead. I still can't believe it.'

'Yes, and what a way to go,' Higgins said, lowering her voice, although it was still comfortably loud enough for me to hear from the upstairs window.

'So, what happened exactly?' Nan asked.

'Electrocuted in the bath apparently. He was in the bath drinking and watching TV, and when the TV fell in with him, that was that. It fried him. What a way to go. He was in there rotting away for two days before they found him. The postman raised the alarm when the smell of the body came through the letterbox. Can you imagine? The police were called out earlier that evening apparently, but they couldn't find anything suspicious, so the official verdict is "death by misadventure", whatever that means. That's what they say anyway.'

Nan crouched down to stroke Ollie, who'd waddled over. 'Is that right?' she said, looking up.

'But I know there's more to it,' Higgins said. 'There's no way it was an accident.'

'No?'

'No. No way. It's not as straightforward as that. Not a chance. I've told the police what really happened, and I know it won't come as a surprise to you.'

'Really? You'd better tell me what happened then.'

Mrs Higgins looked up and down the street, removed her glasses and bent over the gate to talk down to Nan. 'It wasn't an accident. He committed suicide. Think about it, it's obvious really. Sergeant Meadows has retired, so there's nobody to look out for him anymore, and Freya has gone away for God knows what reason. He knew his past was catching up with him, and he couldn't face it. He decided to end it all.'

'Well, well, what about that?' Nan said.

'What are you doing?' Aunty Flo said from behind me.

'Nothing,' I said with a start. 'You made me jump.'

She placed a hand on my shoulder and leant over to get a view from the window. 'The old bat's telling your nan all about the business over the road, no doubt.' She laughed. 'Come on, the snooker's on, come and watch it with me. That Irish player you like is on.'

Closing the window, I said, 'I can't really, I've got some homework to do.'

'Do it later.' She screwed up her face and waved a hand to dismiss the idea. 'Come on, come and watch the snooker.'

We went downstairs and after she'd sent me to the kitchen to make tea, I joined her in the lounge.

Watching Aunty Flo in her armchair, enjoying the snooker with a cigarette and a mug of tea, my thoughts turned to Nan's conversation with Mrs Higgins.

Christmas had passed uneventfully, and I'd returned to school, and after three unremarkable weeks, it struck me how tame the aftermath of Vic's death had been, when my expectations had promised something altogether different.

I'd prepared myself for police interrogations, and probing questions from neighbours and kids at school, all trying to test our resolve, and catch us out, and prove our guilt.

But instead, the fallout had amounted to not much more than casual tittle-tattle over garden fences.

When the police came round to our house to ask some questions, Nan spoke to them alone. Aunty Flo and I had gone to football for the last match before Christmas. The police grilling I'd expected, like the ones you see on TV in a dingy room at the police station with two angry detectives and a tape recorder, turned out to be nothing of the sort.

Nan had said, 'They were very friendly, especially Suzie Greene. I remember when she was a little tot, and I never realised she wanted to be a lady policeman.' Nan invited them in for a cup of tea and they enjoyed some bread pudding left over from the night before. It turns out that Nan knows Suzie's aunty, who's a regular at the pub, so they talked more about her than whether Nan had seen anything suspicious over at Vic's house that night.

Nan said to me afterwards, 'Now we can put it behind us, and move on with our lives,' and it amazed me how easy it had been to do exactly that.

'What did that old cow have to say for herself, then?' Aunty Flo asked when Nan breezed into the lounge.

'You know, the usual stuff. I'm sure you can imagine.'

Aunty Flo threw up her hands. 'Oh, I can't believe he's fluffed it,' she cried out as the crowd on the TV groaned.

Turning to Nan, she answered, 'I can imagine alright, I bet she's been asking the police more questions than they've been asking her, the nosey old bat.'

'She knows everything about everything as usual,' Nan said, 'and she's been doing the police's work for them, apparently. She's told them it wasn't an accident.'

'What's she said then?' Aunty Flo asked with a trace of concern.

'She thinks it was suicide.'

'Suicide,' Aunty Flo laughed.

'She's convinced it was, but she's heard the official verdict is "death by misadventure" as well,' Nan said.

Aunty Flo turned away from the TV screen after the pink ball had rolled into a pocket, and she rested her eyes on her younger sister.

The Irish snooker player chalked his cue and slotted in the black to win the frame, and he now only needed one more for the match.

The cheering crowd recaptured Aunty Flo's attention and she said quietly in my ear, 'There's no stopping him now.'

Nan sat down in her spot on the sofa and picked up her knitting. 'Oh, I almost forgot,' she said, 'Freya's aunty and uncle were over the road earlier while you were at school. They came down to pick up some things and they popped in afterwards.'

'Did they say how Freya is?'

'They said she was alright, but they didn't say too much, really.'

'Did Freya send a message? She must have told them to say something?'

'No, I'm sorry, love. There wasn't a message. I expect Freya wants to make a fresh start and put everything that's happened here behind her.'

'Everything?'

'No, not everything, but you know what I mean. It couldn't have been nice for her living here with him, and now she's got the chance to start a new life where she can be happy.'

'So, what did they say?'

'Hardly anything, really. They had to get away to beat the traffic, and they only popped in to drop something off for you. There's a box out in the kitchen.'

I went quickly to the kitchen where I found a small, brown cardboard box sat next to the bread bin, sealed with several strips of masking tape stuck along the centre of the two cardboard flaps.

I sliced open the tape with a pair of scissors and opened out the lid to find the box full of scrunched up-newspaper. When I pulled out some of the paper, I saw Larry's clock perched on top of an untidy pile of bank notes. I emptied out the rest of the newspaper in the hope of finding a letter or a note, but there was nothing else inside.

Nan shouted from the other room, 'Are you alright, love?'

'Yeah.'

'What's in the box? Bring it through.'

After stuffing everything back inside, I carried the box into the lounge, handed it to Nan and slumped down next to her.

She brushed Ollie off her lap and onto mine. 'But this is Larry's clock?' she said, holding it up to me. 'It's the clock from your grandad's letters. I thought Larry had given it to you. Why did Freya have it?'

'Larry did give it to me,' I said, 'but I gave it to her.'

'Why?'

'I don't know. It just felt like the right thing to do.'

'Well, love,' she said, turning the clock over in her

hands, 'that was a nice thing to do, but I think both Larry and your grandad would like you to have it, really.'

'I know that now,' I said. 'I'm sorry, I didn't realise at the time, but I promise I'll look after it from now on.'

'And what's all this?' Nan pulled out a fistful of cash and held it up to Aunty Flo. Several notes dropped from the bundle as she did so.

'Where did you get that from, Jamie?' Aunty Flo asked.

'I traded the bonds, and then I gave the money to Freya so she could run away from her dad.'

'What? You've already been there?' Aunty Flo asked. 'And you went without me?'

'I went when you were in hospital.'

'And he cashed it there and then, no fuss?'

I nodded.

'This is all from the bonds you got in Oxford?' Nan asked, picking up another clump of money. 'Where did you exchange it?'

'At Roxy's casino in Brewer Street.'

'You went to see Billy Apples?' Nan asked. 'You went there by yourself, and you came out with all this?'

'Yes.'

'And you let him go up there by himself?' Nan said to Aunty Flo.

'I didn't think he'd go up there by himself,' Aunty Flo said. 'I told him to keep them safe in case anything happened to us, and to go up there and cash them in when he was older, and he needed a car or something.'

'Roxy's casino,' Nan said, shaking her head. 'And you brought it home from London on your own?'

'Yes,' I said timidly.

The snooker player powered in a long red and screwed over off the cushion for the black. Applause erupted from the TV, but Aunty Flo had lost interest.

'I can't believe you went there without telling me,' Aunty Flo said. 'What are you going to do with it now, then? It's your money.'

'Put it in the bank and keep it safe,' Nan said, shoving the money back in the box and closing the lid.

'I don't need it,' I said, 'and I've got another idea. Why don't we go on holiday?'

'No, don't be silly,' Nan said. 'Stick it in the bank and you can use it when you're older, for a car or a deposit on a flat or something like that.'

'But I don't want to,' I said. 'Let's go on holiday together. You gave our holiday money to Sita, so let's use this instead. What about Boston?'

'Boston?' they both said together.

'Yes, Boston, to see Uncle Sid. Billy told me he wanted to go with my dad, but they couldn't in the end, but we can go now. We can go to America.'

Nan frowned. 'Billy told you about that?'

'You've always said you'd love to go and see Sid.'

'A long time ago maybe, but not now,' Nan said.

'So can we go?'

'Jamie, don't be ridiculous.' Nan withdrew a cigarette from its packet and lit it. 'We're not about to start gallivanting around the world on planes at our age.'

'We could, you know, Bet,' Aunty Flo said. 'We could go, all of us. We could spend some of that money on a holiday, and there'd still be plenty left for Jamie in the future.'

'Don't be silly, Florence. It's a ridiculous idea. We don't even have passports.'

'We could get passports,' I said.

'Now look what you've done,' Nan said. 'You've given him the idea we could go.'

'Why not, Bet?' Aunty Flo asked. 'Just imagine how much fun it would be. One last adventure. Think back to when we were kids. If someone had said to us we'd have the chance to go to America one day, we would never have believed it. But we can, we can go, we've got that chance now.'

I'd enjoyed Aunty Flo's impassioned speech, but it appeared to have no effect on Nan.

'No, no. It's madness,' she said irritably. 'Stop talking about it. Jamie, go and make some tea, go on.'

Ollie leapt onto Nan's lap as I got up.

I banged around the kitchen and when I brought the tea in, they were watching the snooker in silence.

After I'd set their cups down, I walked over to the fireplace and placed Larry's clock next to the picture of my parents.

I asked Nan, 'Can we keep this here?'

'Of course we can, love.'

Nan stared at the picture and the clock as they sat side by side on the mantlepiece.

I sat down and after some time, I asked her, 'What do you think? Do you like the clock there?'

'Yes, love,' she said, and she seemed to snap out of her trance when she said it, 'yes, it's the perfect place for it.'

The Irish player made a break of 82 and won the match, and to the sound of applause, he was now shaking hands with his opponent and the referee.

For the duration of the break, Nan hadn't knitted a stitch. I ignored the post-match interviews and watched her face instead, until she finally said to Aunty Flo, 'Where is it that Sid lives, Boston?'

'Yeah, I think so. Boston or somewhere near there. He's got that big fancy house. Remember him telling us about it the last time he came over. We could all doss down there for a couple of weeks. He'd love it.'

Nan put her knitting down for a moment before saying, 'Maybe I was a bit hasty. Maybe it would be nice to spend some of that money.'

'Really?' I asked. 'So we can go to Boston?'

'Well, we need to look into it first, but if it's possible, then I don't see why we shouldn't go. We could ask Neil if he fancied it. He's never been abroad either. He might say yes. And we could even ask Larry? The five of us could go.'

'We'd have a great time, Bet,' Aunty Flo said. 'Think about it, we wouldn't have to do any shopping, any cooking, any cleaning, or any washing up.'

'You don't do any of that anyway,' Nan said, but Aunty Flo ignored her and carried on talking.

'Yeah, Sid's wife Daphne, she would do everything for us.'

Nan slurped at her tea. 'I could pop into the travel agent's tomorrow and pick up some passport forms from the post office.'

The back door opened, and Neil plodded in. 'What's for dinner?' he asked as he fell into his chair.

'Bangers and mash, love,' Nan said. 'I've got some of those nice sausages.'

'Thanks, Betty.'

'Guess what, Neil,' Aunty Flo called out, unable to contain her delight. 'We've come into some money, and we're going on holiday. We're going to America, and you're coming with us.'

Neil picked the newspaper off the table and fidgeted around in his armchair to get comfy.

'That's nice,' he said, and he vanished behind *The Daily Mirror*.

27

'This is really important, dear; we can't get this wrong. Are you absolutely certain it won't be a problem?' Aunty Flo's voice strained with concern.

'Yes, Mrs Buchanan. I've checked and double-checked. You're definitely booked in the smoking section of the plane.'

I thought our petite travel agent, who didn't appear to be much older than me, coped admirably with the questions directed across her desk.

Her flame–red hair contrasted with the white-and-green striped uniform she wore and, although she nervously wrapped her curls around her ear from time to time, at no point did she falter with her responses.

'Are you're absolutely certain there's a smoking section?' Aunty Flo asked. 'In The White Hart, they were telling me smoking has been banned.'

'It's all confirmed here,' the young girl said. 'There is talk of a total ban in the future, but there is definitely a smoking section on your plane.'

'I need to talk to you about the food, love,' Nan said. 'Have you ever been to America?'

'No, I've not been, but my friend has.'

'Did she have to eat all that American muck?'

'I guess so.'

'Well, I'm not going to eat hamburgers and hot dogs all day,' Nan said. 'Do you know whether she was able to get some proper English food when she was over there?'

'I'm not sure, Mrs Callaghan.'

'I'm not worried about staying with Sid and Daphne,' Nan said. 'I've told them what food to get, but Sid's going to drive us around Massachusetts and New England in his big van thing, and we're going to be staying in places that are like hotels, but they're called motels. Did your friend go to a motel?'

'Yes, I think so,' the travel agent said.

'Can we get English food there?'

'I'm not sure, but I think you'll be fine, Mrs Callaghan. America is very popular with our customers; we have sent lots of people to all parts of the country, and I'm sure you'll find something that you like.'

Larry, standing behind Nan's chair, gave her a nudge. 'You won't have to cook for two weeks, Betty, or wash up.'

'Or clean,' Neil chipped in.

Nan broke out into a smile. 'Well, that does sound quite nice.'

'And look at this beach, Nan,' I said, twisting the brochure round for her to see.

'And look at that bar,' Aunty Flo said excitedly.

'It does look very nice,' Nan said. 'I still can't believe we're going. You've probably guessed, love, but none of us have ever done this before.'

'I've been told New England is a beautiful place,' the

travel agent said, 'and I'm sure you'll have a wonderful time when you're there.'

'So,' Larry said, 'can you go over what we do when we get to the airport again?'

The young travel agent politely worked through our questions for the next 15 minutes, before Aunty Flo made the final payment by handing over a carrier bag full of fifty- and twenty-pound notes.

'Are you excited, Nan?' I asked as we walked out of the shop into the drizzling rain on Northbrook Street. 'I'm sure the food will be great.'

'I can't wait, love, and I'm sure the food will be just fine,' she said, putting her arm around me. 'But I'll pack a suitcase of biscuits just in case.'

We arrived home in Neil's van to find Dr Reynolds parked outside waiting. The doctor climbed out of his car and greeted us, but declined to come inside out of the drizzle.

'I can't stop, Betty, sorry. I'm already running late today, but I wanted to tell you in person. I received a phone call from the hospital yesterday afternoon, the hospital where they've been running tests on Bill's body. They've finished with him now.'

'Did they find out anything?' Nan asked.

'I don't know,' Dr Reynolds said apologetically. 'It's not something they divulge, I'm afraid, but I do know they were extremely grateful to him, and you, for allowing the research. The reason I'm here is to tell you that Bill's body has been released, so you can now have the funeral.'

'Thank you for telling me, Doctor. I'll give Mr Rossi a call.'

'No need, I've already phoned him for you. He'll be in touch on Monday to discuss the details.'

'Thank you, Doctor,' Nan said, as he got back into his car.

Mr Rossi called early on Monday morning and arrangements were made for the following Friday.

Grandad's funeral was very different from Sir Richard de Savery's. No crowds, no church, no formal ceremony, or religious formalities.

'You knew him well enough,' Nan had said when Mr Rossi asked, 'he wouldn't want any of that stuff.'

When Friday afternoon came, the five of us met Mr Rossi at Thatcham Cemetery.

We found him waiting up in the top left corner of the cemetery, under the canopy of a grand old oak tree that offered some much-needed shade from the scorching July sun.

We walked up together, and Mr Rossi welcomed us solemnly in front of the new shiny grey headstone he'd arranged.

I tried to focus on the black writing carved into the stone, "William Lionel Callaghan 7 February 1925 to 26 September 1986 Loving Husband, Dad and Grandad", but my eyes kept flitting back to the space above it, deliberately left blank for a future inscription.

While Larry chatted to Mr Rossi, Nan placed a bouquet of red roses on the raised mound of earth and then pointed out positions of other friends and neighbours who had already found their way there. I knew my parents were buried at a cemetery in London and although she didn't mention it, I knew she was thinking about them.

The new suit Neil had bought especially for the day appeared to be aggravating him. He constantly tugged at the sleeves and fiddled with the cuffs of the shirt underneath. It occurred to me that he had never met Grandad, but even so, the thought of Neil not being with us for the occasion seemed completely absurd.

Mr Rossi positioned himself at the head of the grave and coughed to draw our attention. He straightened his black tie, removed a folded note from his inside jacket pocket, and he began to read.

The short Italian man with tight grey curly hair spoke in a soft, slightly accented English. His words swirled around with the gentle breeze and the rustling of leaves, and it became immediately obvious that Nan had prepared the note.

He described Grandad's early life in London, growing up through the Depression and then working on the buses as his father had before him.

I felt Larry's trembling hand rest on my shoulder when the narrative turned to the war. The account revealed the horrors encountered by the young 19-year-old on the beaches of Normandy, his journey across France, Belgium, and Germany until victory in Europe was secured, and then his final postings in Berlin and Burma.

I didn't know, until Mr Rossi read it out, that Grandad started boxing when he got home from the war and he went on to be the middleweight champion for North West London with thirteen undefeated bouts.

But if the revelations that Grandad was a boxing champion had shocked me, the following passage came as no surprise. We learned how Nan, concerned with his health, asked him to give up boxing and that evening he jogged around to his trainer's flat; to tell him he'd had his last fight.

'For their first date together,' Mr Rossi said, 'on a cold and foggy November Saturday, they caught the bus, and Bill took Betty to the cafe in Regent's Park. He later confessed to taking her there because it was cheap, and he didn't have the money to go anywhere else.

'But the date was perfect,' Mr Rossi continued, 'and walking up Primrose Hill together later that day, Betty already knew they would marry and be together forever.'

Nan had been weeping and dabbing at her eyes with tissues, but at this point she broke down and abruptly twisted her shuddering head into Aunty Flo's shoulder.

The hand on my shoulder patted anxiously and I suspected Larry sensed the worst had yet to come.

Mr Rossi turned the page. 'Bill and Betty married shortly after the war and, soon after, were blessed with a beautiful baby boy, Regan. He was a happy, contented child who grew into a handsome, intelligent and charming young man that Bill and Betty were very proud of.'

I saw Nan's left leg buckle. She lurched sideways, almost dragging her sister to the ground with her, but Aunty Flo managed to hold on and keep them both upright.

His hand slipped from my shoulder and Larry left my side to help. He gathered his arms around the two women and ushered them to the bench at the side of the grave.

When the group had settled, Mr Rossi wiped his brow with a white handkerchief and the eulogy went on. 'Bill and Betty were delighted to receive Angela Baker into the family when she married Regan and more good news followed with the birth of their darling grandson, Jamie. Sadly, their joy was short-lived and it was a distressing time for Bill, Betty and Jamie when Regan and his young wife Angie died in tragic circumstances in a car crash.'

Aunty Flo's face creased with emotion when Mr Rossi said it, but I'd already worked out long before that her Conor had in some way caused the crash and yet survived it.

'Bill struggled to cope at times,' Mr Rossi continued, 'and they moved out of London to Thatcham thanks to his good friend from the war, Larry Baxter. At this time, Bill's illness became increasingly worse and he would suffer for the rest of his life, although he found great comfort in raising his beautiful grandson, Jamie, whom he adored.'

I walked around the bench and put my arms around Nan, and she cradled my head as we sobbed together.

Some of Mr Rossi's last few sentences escaped me, but I do remember him describing Grandad's love of boxing and how he wanted to help others with his condition by donating his body for research.

After he'd finished reading the note, Mr Rossi folded it neatly in half and slid it back into his jacket pocket.

Aunty Flo wandered over to Grandad's gravestone and tapped the top of it tenderly. 'He was a good man, Bet,' she said. 'He was a good man. Come on, let's go and have a drink.'

We walked down the cemetery path to Larry's car, Mr Rossi in front with the five of us behind, clutching on to one another with Nan propped up in the middle.

Nan thanked Mr Rossi, who politely said his goodbyes and went off to see his next grieving family.

We drove to The Swan and spent the rest of the

afternoon sat on a wooden bench in the garden, watching the trains pass through Thatcham station.

Four elderly men, sipping at pints of cider a few tables over, recognised Aunty Flo and waved to acknowledge her.

Larry brought us drinks and crisps on a tray and, as expected, Aunty Flo took centre stage. She made us laugh with stories of the tricks she'd played on Bill when he first started courting her sister.

'I told him Betty had always wanted to go to Royal Ascot,' she said with a grin.

'That's right,' Nan remembered. 'I didn't know what he was on about when he said we were going. He was so pleased with the idea. Then you joined us at the bus stop with some nonsense about being a chaperone.'

'I'd been desperate to go for years,' Aunty Flo said, 'and I bet you had more fun with me there, didn't you?'

'That's what you kept on telling us,' Nan replied. 'But we did have a lot of fun.'

The stories of their youth flowed with the drinks, and they eventually turned to the war, where Larry, as Grandad had always done, skilfully avoided answering the questions.

'Can we get the suitcase down from the attic?' I asked. 'And look through the pictures of you, Aunty Flo and Grandad when you were young?'

'Yes, love,' Nan said. 'Of course we can. Just to prove we weren't always old.'

The barman came outside whistling and collecting the empty glasses. As he filled his tray, Nan said, 'I think it's time. Come on, let's go home.'

Neil drove us home and, at Nan's insistence, Larry came in to join us for dinner.

Nan put on her pinny and started in the kitchen, while the others moved the dining room chairs out to the garden where a family of sparrows had joined the blackbirds up in the conifer trees.

I came out of the sun and into the cool of the lounge to find Stan and Ollie curled up and panting on the settee. Ollie's eye had at last started to show signs of improvement.

Before switching on the TV, I went over to the mantelpiece to see Grandad's clock and my parents' wedding photo.

Sunlight from the window filled with floating particles of dust obscured the faded yellow image, so I held up the picture to bring it into focus.

'It's a nice photo, isn't it?' Nan said over my shoulder.

I turned and said, 'Yes, they look happy.'

'Come and sit down, love,' she said. 'I've made you a cup of tea.'

She placed two cups on the table, took the photo from me, and perched on the sofa in her usual place.

Her pinafore crumbled as she sank into position and when she smiled, I noticed a smudge of flour across her cheek.

'Come and join me,' she said, and at the side of the sofa I saw a photo album I'd never seen before.

She lingered on the picture and, when I sat next to her, she handed it back to me.

'You're ready, love,' she said. 'Let me tell you about them.'